Three Songs by Hank Williams

Three Songs by Hank Williams

Short Stories

by Calvin Wharton

TURNSTONE PRESS

Three Songs by Hank Williams
copyright © Calvin Wharton 2002

Turnstone Press
607-100 Arthur Street
Artspace Building
Winnipeg, MB
R3B 1H3 Canada
www.TurnstonePress.com

All rights reserved. No part of this book may be reproduced or transmitted in any form or by any means—graphic, electronic or mechanical—without the prior written permission of the publisher. Any request to photocopy any part of this book shall be directed in writing to Cancopy (Canadian Copyright Licensing Agency), Toronto.

Turnstone Press gratefully acknowledges the assistance of The Canada Council for the Arts, the Manitoba Arts Council, the Government of Canada through the Book Publishing Industry Development Program and the Government of Manitoba through the Department of Culture, Heritage and Tourism, Arts Branch for our publishing activities.

Cover photograph: "Texas Highway" by Donovan Reese
Cover design: Kirk Warren
Interior design: Sharon Caseburg
Printed and bound in Canada by Friesens for Turnstone Press.

"I'm So Lonesome I Could Cry" written by Hank Williams, Sr., ©1949 (Renewed 1977) Acuff-Rose Music, Inc. and Hiriam Music for the USA, World outside USA controlled by Acuff-Rose Music, Inc. All rights reserved. Used by Permission. Do not duplicate.
"Long Gone Lonesome Blues" written by Hank Williams, Sr., ©1950 (Renewed 1978) Acuff-Rose Music, Inc. and Hiriam Music for the USA, World outside USA controlled by Acuff-Rose Music, Inc. All rights reserved. Used by Permission. Do not duplicate.
"Why Don't You Love Me" written by Hank Williams, Sr., ©1950 (Renewed 1977) Acuff-Rose Music, Inc. and Hiriam Music for the USA, World outside USA controlled by Acuff-Rose Music, Inc. All rights reserved. Used by Permission. Do not duplicate.

National Library of Canada Cataloguing in Publication Data

Wharton, Calvin, 1952-
Three songs by Hank Williams
ISBN 0-88801-270-5
I. Title
PS8595.H27T47 2002   C813'.54   C2002-910056-9
PR9199.3.W4276T47 2002

For Lian and Sean, my two favourite songs.

Acknowledgements

How can I possibly thank all the many people without whom this book, etc.? I'll name the ones I can think of and hope that if I've left anyone out, they'll forgive me. My gratitude to Tom Wayman and Noel Hudson for years of enthusiastic encouragement and support; to George McWhirter, Linda Svendson and Keith Maillard for their guidance and suggestions; to Guy Vanderhaeghe and the workshop at Booming Ground; to my editor, Wayne Tefs; and to my friends and colleagues at Douglas College. Also, of course, thanks to Lian Zhang and Sean Wharton, who provided the familial infrastructure, as well as commentary along the way.

Grateful acknowledgement to the following publications, where some of these stories first appeared: "Something to Say" in *Dandelion*; "Three Songs by Hank Williams" in *Descant*; "They Almost Quench Your Thirst," "Glass Houses," and "Bisecting Mirror" in *Geist*; and "Paper Covers Rock" in *Pottersfield Porfolio*.

Contents

Something to Say	3
Three Songs by Hank Williams	13
Constraints of Gravity	33
They Almost Quench Your Thirst	41
Wrapped in Blue	43
Glass Houses	55
Chicken Man	57
A Thing of Beauty	79
The End of Water	89
Paper Covers Rock	101
So Great to Be Alive	107
Bisecting Mirror	117
As Do the Birds	119

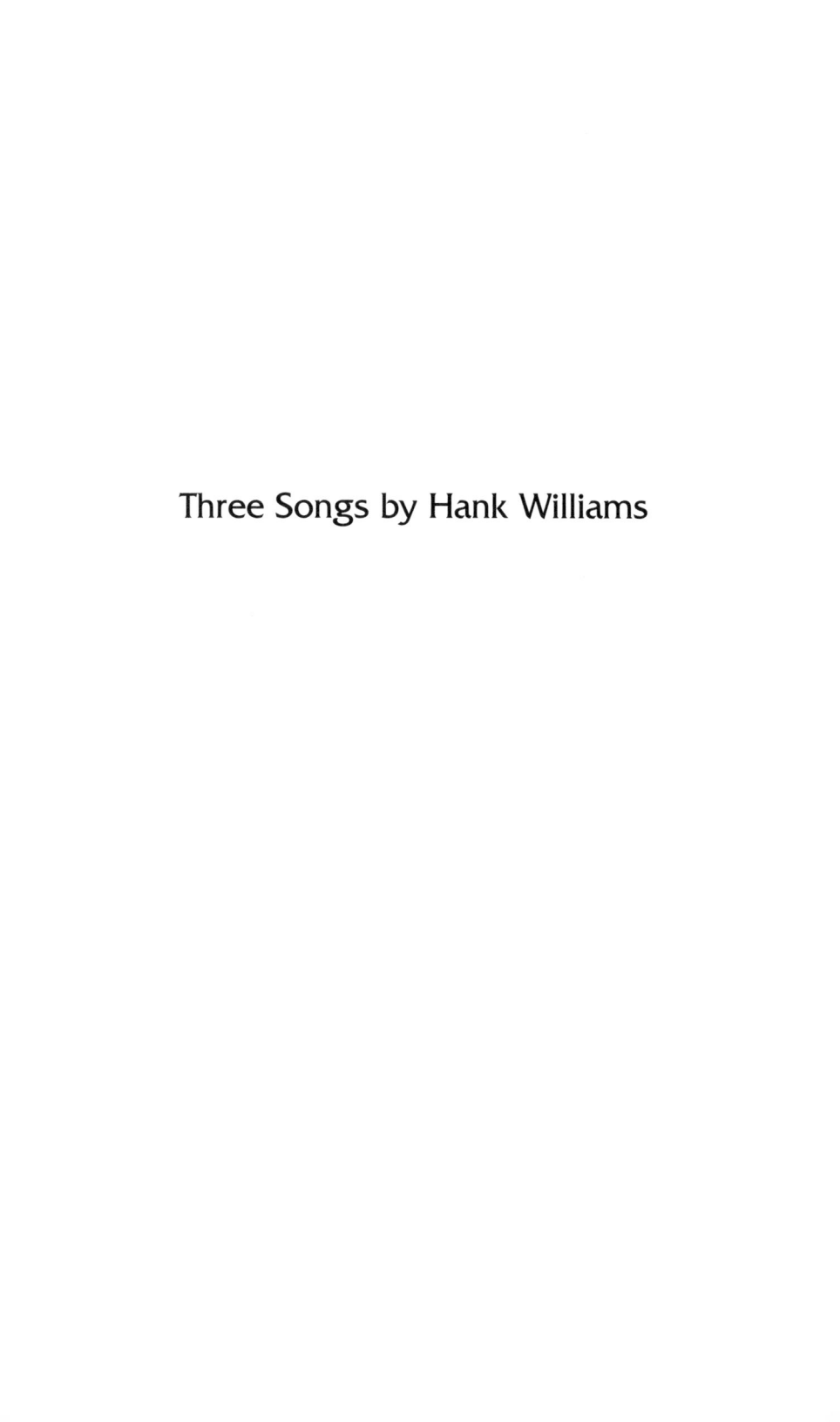

Three Songs by Hank Williams

Something to Say

I saw my father today for the first time since he died last May. He was driving a yellow three-ton with the windows rolled down, even though this last week of October has been cold and rainy. I noticed he'd let his silvery hair and beard grow a bit longer than his regular military-trim cut, and he looked good in that black T-shirt. I was in my car beside him at a traffic light and I had a fairly clear side view of him. I wondered if he'd picked up the tan over the summer and noticed how he'd grown muscular again, after so many years of sliding downhill, health-wise. He didn't seem like a man who'd need to ride to the Legion on a battery-powered scooter.

Darcy was in his car seat, behind me. "Look, Darce, there's Grandpa," I said.

"Grandpa," he said. "At hospital." He's only two years old, but he can already talk quite well.

"No, right up there in the yellow truck," I said, and pointed. My dad was smoking a cigarette and kept flicking the ash out the window. He was laughing and speaking to someone in the cab.

"Truck," Darcy said, but I could see in the rear-view that he was focussed on his feet braced against the seat in front of him.

When the light changed, I went through the intersection and pulled ahead of the rest of the traffic. I slowed to turn left onto Mary Hill Road, but when the big three-ton went rattling past, I stepped on it, swung into the lane behind him and followed up the hill.

Dad never baulked at driving. When I was a kid he'd get a bug up his ass to visit Uncle Russ, his younger brother, and right after work on a Friday he'd come home with a case of beer, the bottles pinging together under his arm, announcing we were going to Quesnel for the weekend. Mom only complained if he'd been drinking already. Otherwise, she seemed happy to spend eight hours in the car just to get out of Vancouver for a change. I usually didn't mind, but nobody asked me, anyway.

One Easter weekend he and Uncle Russ spent three days playing crib, adding to the scores they'd been keeping for years, into the millions of points. Standing, watching them, I realized their game had evolved into a kind of ritual, a religious ceremony for them. I knew never to interfere in the middle of a hand, especially if my dad was getting skunked. But this time he noticed me hanging around, and carefully set his fanned-out cards face-down on the table. "Oland," he said, "haven't you got homework to do?"

"No," I said. "I did it in the car yesterday."

"Then get me and Uncle Russ another beer." He never asked my sister to do anything. She could even come and sit on his knee for a while, but before long he'd send her off to play with the cousins. He said that since I was older, I had to take some responsibility.

The next morning I got up early just to hold the wooden cribbage board in my lap. I ran my fingers around the long rows of parallel holes and took the metal pegs out of the little compartment on the underside of the board. But I made sure I was done with it before anyone else woke.

On Easter Monday, after Aunt Beth, Mom and us kids got back from Mass, he had our car packed for the trip home. I never heard him complain about the long drive or bad traffic—unusual, since he complained about pretty well everything else.

I guess the notion of seeing my dad finally caught Darcy's interest, because he started singing a nonsense song about going to see Grandpa. "Sing, Daddy," he insisted, then slid back into the melody, which sounded a lot like "Twinkle, Twinkle, Little Star," his favourite tune. "Grandpa, Grandpa, at the hospital," I crooned along with him. We often used this singing game to pass time in the car together. One of us would spot something interesting, then make up a verse for it.

If Colleen was with us and tried to join in, Darcy cut her off pretty quick. "No, Mama. Daddy sing, not Mama." She and I both considered it funny, but I never laughed at him when he did this. He was clear this was something only for him and me, and no matter how cute I might find the situation, it also made me teary-eyed when I gave it some thought.

Most of the time I spent alone with my dad was silent. He used to get me to help him while he worked on cars out in the garage. About the only thing he'd say to me was, "Hand me a nine-sixteenths box-end," or, "Swing the trouble light over by the alternator." If I asked him about what he was doing, he'd give me a short answer and keep working. The main thing I got out of this was a true hatred for country and western music, which he always had playing on the radio. Even today, if I hear Hank Snow or Marty Robbins start up on some oldies station, I feel depressed.

When I was eleven or twelve, he decided to earn some extra money fixing up old cars and selling them. On weekends he'd drag me off to wrecking yards out in Surrey to look for parts. Hardly more than a few sentences would pass between us on the way there. At the wreckers', he'd let me wander on my own through the rows of rusting and crumpled vehicles. Once, I came around an old Dodge Fargo pickup with the front end accordioned back to a shattered windshield. Dad was standing, looking at a mid-fifties Chevy behind it. "Find anything?" I asked, and I think I startled him because he jumped a bit.

"This is just like the first car we had," he said. "I sold it when you were still a baby, so you probably don't remember it."

Well, of course I had no memory of this, but I really wanted to. "Yeah," I said, my face up close to the passenger side window. "I think I do remember riding in a car like this." I could see his face reflected in the glass, and I'm sure he smiled.

I was two cars back from the yellow truck, waiting for the swing span on the Pitt River Bridge to close. Traffic stacked up in both directions until the guy in the shed at the centre of the bridge could bring the sections back together. What a job, I thought. Sit around for hours in case a boat comes along, then stop and perform in front of dozens of impatient drivers. Maybe it would feel great to have that many people hanging on you and have a good reason for it.

Below us, a big green tug motored slowly downstream, its wake widening out behind it like a veil. "Tugboat," I said, and wondered if Darcy could see it.

"Why, Daddy?" he asked. At this point, *why* is his standard comment on every new situation.

"Tugboats pull things, like logs or big ships, behind them on the water," I explained. "They work hard."

He turned sideways in his seat to watch, a look of concentration on his face, like he was trying to remember something. His fuzzy straight hair stood around his head the way light circles the heads of the innocent in religious paintings. I had an urge to reach over and touch him, but I didn't want to disturb his thoughts.

In my last year of high school, the sawmill shut down and Dad lost his job. He'd started at Western Forest Products on the green chain before I was born, and over the years worked his way up to foreman. I could tell it was tough for him to lose such a major part of his identity, but the opportunity to talk to him about it never seemed to come.

In those days, people could still find work if they wanted it, even someone in his early forties like my dad. None of the other mills around were hiring, so he ended up getting on in the service department of BowMac car and truck rentals on Broadway. He was relieved to find something he at least enjoyed, but he regretted his loss of status. I overheard him talking to my mom one day. "I'm just a grease monkey, Meg," he said, "a goddamn grease monkey."

Unfortunately, it wasn't a great time for me, either. I wasn't sure what I was going to do when school was finished. I thought I might want to work a while, and save some money to travel around Europe. When I mentioned this to Dad, he put down the newspaper he'd been reading and said, "You'll be going to military college. Royal Roads. I've already sent off for an application."

His certainty stunned me, because we'd never really discussed the issue before, and I realized he'd made a lot of plans for me without any consultation. I wasn't against the idea of going to college, but I wanted to wait a year. It was difficult for me, but I looked him in the eye and said calmly, "You don't have a clue who I am. I'll never go to military college."

"Why not?" he asked. "It's a quality education and it's free. The problem with you is you can't stand anybody telling you what to do."

"At least you got that much right."

He stood up to face me and I noticed we were the same height. "Well," he said, "it's goddamned time you started facing the facts of life."

"Maybe your truth and mine just don't match," I said.

He stared at me, and for a moment what I saw in his eyes was more like fear or uncertainty than anger. "Facts are facts," he said.

Mom eventually intervened and said we should all think about it for a while and talk it out later. But I wouldn't budge on this one. I went out that day and applied for part-time at the local Safeway. When summer vacation started, I worked as many hours as they'd let me. I saved most of what I earned, then cleared out my savings and flew to London on my birthday in August. Mom and Dad drove me to the airport, but he said his goodbyes in the car. He claimed he didn't want to pay the fool's tax they put on parking fees out there. My mom came in with me and saw me through the boarding gate while Dad circled around the airport road.

Along the highway in Maple Ridge, the yellow three-ton turned into the White Spot parking lot. I followed, and stayed in the car while my dad parked the truck. Darcy got excited when he saw the familiar building—he and I often went there on Saturday afternoons for a treat. "French fries ketchup," he shouted. I smiled and watched two men walk from the truck toward the restaurant. My dad seemed shorter and had a slight limp, but he looked filled-out again. His partner appeared to be younger than him, with freckles and hair the colour of a new penny—the kind of guy Dad would have nicknamed Red. My dad held the door open for the other man, like I knew he would, and they went inside.

I parked in another part of the lot and turned the engine off. Across the street, some kids were horsing around on skateboards. I had the sensation of floating sideways, like the low-level clouds shouldering their way along, underneath the darker ones above.

"Well, Darcy," I said, "what do you think? Should we go in?"

"French fries ketchup," he said.

The last time I saw him, he'd been in the Royal Columbian for three and a half months already. They'd hacked off his left foot and his right leg below the knee because it was the only way to stop the spread of gangrene from his diabetes. When I got to his room, he was asleep, breath moving in and out of his lungs like dry leaves dragged across sandpaper. I introduced myself to his new roommate, Ernie, and pulled up a chair next to Dad's bed.

I wondered if I should wake him, but sat and watched him sleep. He looked shrunken and diminished, like a balloon that's been slowly losing air. When he woke up, he was looking straight at me—his eyes opened and he began to talk as if we'd been in the middle of some long conversation. "So, Oland," he said, "how's that grandson of mine?"

"He's doing great, Dad. I would have brought him, but I didn't have time to go pick him up. How are you?"

"About as well as could be expected." He shifted a bit and the blanket fell away from the bandage where his foot used to be. "It's healing really well, they say. Vraybeck said I might even be able to get an artificial foot some day."

I didn't ask him how he felt about having no feet, or if he worried whether he'd ever get out of the hospital. On the way over, I'd imagined a conversation that grew to fill in the blank spaces we'd cultivated between us. Instead, I told him how Darcy had started riding his tricycle around the driveway, talked generally about how things were going at work and other trivial matters.

"Hey, son," he said. "Would you mind going downstairs and getting me a can of diet Coke? I'm so damn thirsty all the time." He pointed to the table beside his bed. "There's some money in that drawer."

He watched me pick up his wallet; underneath it was an old black and white photo—a picture of him with a baby in his arms, standing beside what I knew by then was the '55 Chevy he'd owned. When I looked at him, he quickly turned his eyes away. "Your mother found that the other day and brought it in. She thought I'd get a kick out of seeing it."

"That me you're holding?"

"A little peanut," he answered.

I set the photo carefully back in the drawer. "If you had a car like that nowadays, it'd be worth a fortune," I said.

I expected him to start talking about cars and how much they'd changed, but he just lay back and nodded. "Better get me two cans," he said.

A big chunk of my visiting time that day, much like on other days, was occupied by a trip to the cafeteria in the basement. When I got back, he was chatting with Ernie, who used to work for the post office in Yorkton, where my dad grew up. Dad kept telling me things about this guy whom I'd only just met, kept trying to get me involved in a conversation with him. Later, when Ernie went for a walk around the ward, Dad complained about his snoring. "Curly-headed Christ," he said, "his first night I thought there was someone in here with a chainsaw." I laughed, and noticed when he blinked, how his eyelids were like parchment.

Ten days later, he died from a blockage in his coronary artery. No one had suspected his heart was that far gone.

Although he was big enough to walk, I carried Darcy into the restaurant in the crook of my left arm. My dad was sitting by the window, his back to the entrance. I made my way down the aisle between the rows of booths, ignoring the questioning look of the hostess beside the Please Wait to be Seated sign. My knees felt like bubble gum. I stopped just behind him; they were drinking coffee and he was lighting a cigarette.

"Excuse me," I said. The man with the red hair motioned to him, upwards with his eyes, and he turned around to face me. It wasn't him, of course. The mouth was wrong, the nose too flat and the eyes were watery blue instead of an intense hazel. But he could have been a relative, he was that close.

"Can I help you?" he asked. The two of them stared at me, waiting for me to speak.

There were things I wanted to say, needed to tell him. My mouth felt dry and my face burned. "Sorry," I said. "I made a mistake. I thought you were someone I had to talk to." I stepped back and headed for the door.

"Do I know you?" he called after me. "Are you someone I know?"

As soon as Darcy realized we were leaving the restaurant, he started howling. Somehow, I made it out to the car and got him strapped into his car seat; he must have been confused. "French fries ketchup, Daddy," he protested.

"Next time, son," I said. "Next time." And all the way home, I apologized to him, words pouring out of me like water.

Three Songs
by Hank Williams

1. Like Yesterday

> I went down to the river to watch the fish swim by,
> but I got to the river, so lonesome I wanted to die,
> and then I jumped in the river,
> but the doggone river was dry.
>
> —*Long Gone Lonesome Blues*

The unobstructed sun rose from the desert, illuminating him in the opal heart morning outside El Centro, California. Merchant Best stood beside the highway, a cheap, vinyl suitcase at his feet on the dusty shoulder. In his hand, a cigarillo—vanilla-cream—a gift from the driver who had given him a ride out to the edge of the city. Traffic was almost zero, so far, so early, but it didn't matter. Normally, he was impatient, couldn't stand to stand still. But in the past month his psychological metabolism had slowed to a pace he couldn't have imagined possible.

Three weeks on the road, he thought. Twenty-one days since meltdown on the West Coast, his version. He had read in Lao Tzu: "A good runner leaves no tracks," and this had become his motto. He felt pleased with himself, his escape and the shape of his new life. In the moment of admiring both the horizon and his inner real estate, he heard a voice. Earthly, not celestial.

"Got an extra smoke?"

He turned to face a leathery walking-stick of a man, spiky grey hair exploding from the crest of his head. He wore two sets of clothing, one on top of the other, greasy brown nylon jacket with its collar turned up into the bristles at the apex of neck and jaw. "Where'd you come from?" Merchant asked.

The man smiled, big yellow teeth with a couple missing in the back, and stuck out his hand. "Slim's the name, and pleased to meet you."

Merchant shook that hand, dry and papery but with a noticeably strong grip. "I've got some Canadian cigarettes, if that's okay," he said.

"I don't care what kind they are, long as they ain't been soaked in piss. I never smoke nothing that's been in a urinal, though some will. That's where I draw the line." Slim took the offered package, helped himself to one, then reached deep into the pocket of his polyester trousers to extract a single wooden match. As he exhaled, coughing slightly, he looked down the road, away from the city. "So where you headed, Merchant Best?"

"How do you know my name?"

"It's on that card," Slim said, nodding at the handle of the suitcase. Merchant's name was printed on the red, white and blue rectangle of paper from the bus across the border (he'd heard the crossing guards wouldn't let him through if they knew he was planning to hitchhike). But the writing was small and the card, tiny.

"You must have pretty good eyes."

Slim shrugged, then looked at him again, waiting for an answer.

"I'm going to Phoenix, then maybe into Mexico."

"Ah, Phoenix, Arizona, where the sun never stops shining and each day's as good as the one before. Got somewhere to stay there?"

Merchant lied, "Yeah, I've got friends expecting me."

Slim took a last drag of smoke, then carefully pinched the burning end from the cigarette and tucked the butt into an inside pocket of his outer jacket. "Well, I'm going to go get some breakfast. You eat yet?" Merchant nodded. "Too bad, I was going to demonstrate my bumming skills. When I first hit the road—this was years ago—I met up with a fellow named R. Dean Webster. R. Dean taught me how to survive. First thing he said was, 'Slim, if you want to ride the rails, you've got to learn how to bum.' Maybe if we cross paths again some time, I'll show you then."

Slim headed down the road toward a Dairy Queen. Merchant was happy to be on his own again, but somehow the clear gem-like quality of the morning had changed and he could feel a familiar impatience edging his perspective.

When he saw the '57 Buick, big as a hovercraft, coming toward him, he thought there wasn't much chance of getting a ride; even from a distance, he could tell this was a restored classic. Whoever owned a car like that wouldn't pick up hitchhikers, he thought, but the mint green and chrome juggernaut stopped just beyond him. The driver's arm waved to him out the window, so he grabbed his suitcase and ran to the car's passenger side.

"I'm going to Phoenix, man," the driver shouted over loud Mexican radio music. "Throw your suitcase in the back seat."

Merchant climbed in, amazed at his good luck: a ride all the way to Phoenix. "This is great," he said, seeing his benefactor clearly for the first time. "You're going straight through to where I want to go." The young man behind the wheel smiled and pulled the huge car back onto the highway. His dark hair was shaved up the sides and short on top. One ear was adorned with a plain hoop, while a plastic cowboy with a lariat hung from the other. The sleeves of his white T-shirt were rolled up, revealing a tattoo of an arrow suspended on its way to a black and red target.

"Nice car," Merchant said. "Did you do the restoration yourself?" The Buick was a few years older than he, but the leather seats, the padded dash—even the steering wheel—seemed brand new.

"Shit, no," the driver said. "This is my mom's car. I don't have time for that kind of stuff." He turned the sound down on the radio. "My name's Zone."

Large signs at the Arizona border warned against bringing fruit into the state from California. Merchant thought about the sack of oranges tucked under his seat and when Zone told the border inspector that he had no fruit in the car, Merchant just stared straight ahead. A few miles past the station, Zone laughed and said to give him an orange. Merchant laughed with him and ate one, too. But half an hour later, when the state trooper swung out from a roadside rest stop and began to follow them, he wondered how serious these people might get about inter-state citrus smuggling. The instant he heard the siren, he lost track of any possible humour in the matter.

"Oh, oh," Zone said. "Looks like the bear is interested in us. I sure hope my mom didn't report the car."

"What do you mean?" Merchant asked. He'd been thinking oranges.

"Well, she didn't really say I could borrow it. Shit, she hardly uses it and the one time I ask her for a favour she turns into a dark cloud of not-a-chancism."

Zone carefully pulled over to the shoulder, but the trooper's car shot past and hurtled down the highway, disappearing into the sunburned desert horizon. "Hey, we're lucky," the young man said. "He's got other fires to put out."

"Lucky?" Merchant said. "We both could have been in trouble."

"Don't freak out, man, this always happens. I'm prepared for it."

And Merchant had to admit to himself that the younger man looked pretty calm.

"Vancouver. It's in Canada, north of Seattle," Merchant explained. "A watery place. Nothing like the desert."

"I was in Portland once to buy some pot. I guess that's as close as I've been. So why Phoenix?"

"My wife's there. At least, I think she is. About a year ago Doris got involved with a cluster of assorted nuts called the Church of Primary Order. They believe that everything is made up of the same basic stuff. Including people. So we're all part of the same person and our relationships with each other are really relationships with ourselves. I think it's just a rationalization for indiscriminate fucking." Merchant watched the desert change perspective out the side window. "Anyway, we didn't agree about the nature of this so-called church, and about a month ago I came home to a note that said she was off to work for the cause. Don't wait up."

"What makes you think she's in Phoenix?"

"That's the main centre for this operation. Doris talked a

lot about how important it was for her to make the pilgrimage. She kept telling me I should open my eyes to something besides ways to make easy money. So I have; but I still think this Primary Order crap is simply a kind of new cult boot camp."

"Well, friend," Zone said, "I hope you are open-minded, because I've got to take a little detour. I've got something to deliver." He slowed the Buick, moved over into a left-turn bay and took a narrow, unpaved road north through the rust-coloured landscape. Merchant wondered what was being delivered and where. He imagined the trunk filled with shrink-wrapped bricks of marijuana, something he'd seen only in news reports. But it was too late to complain; he was in the car and the car was moving. He thought of asking to be let out, but didn't want to take his chances hitching in the sand with nothing but clumps of desert grass, sage and knee-high barrel cactus to keep him company. It was already past noon and there hadn't been a lot of traffic on the highway; he certainly wasn't prepared to spend the night there. He began to wonder if he'd ever get to Phoenix.

"Don't worry," Zone said. "I'll get you where you're going."

"There's more than one way to interpret that statement," Merchant said. Zone smiled and kept driving.

Zone eventually swung down a drive that ended at a trio of wooden buildings in a grove of mesquite and Jerusalem-thorn. Perry, who Merchant thought looked a lot like Slim—tall and whip-like—came smiling out of the largest of the three structures. Zone had explained that this homestead was built for the 1953 western, *Arizona Manhunt*, starring Rex Allen, one of the last of the singing cowboys. Perry had played a small role in the film, and had sought this place out after a weekend on LSD in the early seventies.

"Hey, Zone," he shouted, "nice car." His canvas jeans, faded shirt and battered Stetson, in this setting, made him look like one of the grizzled old sidekicks from the Saturday matinees of Merchant's childhood.

"My mom's. I'm on my way to Phoenix; this is Merchant. He's going with me." As Perry shook hands with Merchant, Zone went around to the back of the car and opened the trunk. "Look what I brought you," he said.

In the trunk was a handmade, plywood box shaped like a coffin, only shorter and flatter. Zone undid the clasps on one side and lifted the lid. Inside was an acoustic guitar, with mother of pearl inlay on the fret board and a series of painted figures chasing each other infinitely around the sound hole. Perry smiled but didn't act surprised. "A real beauty, Zone." He put his right foot up on the Buick's bumper and rested the instrument across the top of his leg. "Where'd you find this?"

"My cousin made it. He lives in Mexicali. Owed me some money and gave me the guitar instead."

They went inside for lunch, then sat the afternoon away drinking smoky moonshine. As the day advanced, Merchant began to feel comfortable in that place. Maybe it was the drink, but he felt as if he was right where he ought to be. He stopped worrying about Phoenix.

That evening, after supper, the three sat on the porch and Perry retold the story of how he came to be living there. "I wasn't surprised to find the buildings still here," he said. "The desert air is a natural preservative, something the ancient Egyp-shines took advantage of to help keep their mummies in good shape." Perry tuned the guitar as he spoke, and danced his fingers over the fret board. "It didn't take much to make the place livable," he said. "I've been here since—about twenty years, now."

Perry picked out the melody to what Merchant recognized as a Hank Williams song—"Long Gone Lonesome Blues."

"You know," Perry said, "I played steel guitar for two weeks with Hank's band the same year we made that movie. The regular man, Shorty Baird, got into a little trouble with his girlfriend and Hank needed a short-term replacement. Seems like all the really important things in my life happened back then. But I remember them like it was yesterday."

The sun had been swallowed by the horizon, draining the brilliant colours from the sky and the landscape. In the dark, Merchant looked up into the heavens and breathed deeply. He noticed the air was rich with the smell of melon.

"That's the saguaro cactus flowers," Perry explained. "They only open at night."

Merchant felt the fragrant air enter his lungs with a sweetness, as if he'd been holding his breath under water. Beside him, Perry began to sing.

2. Slim

> I hear that lonesome whippoorwill; she sounds too blue to fly.
> The midnight train is whining low; I'm so lonesome I could cry.
> Did you ever see a night so long, as time goes crawling by?
> The moon just went behind the clouds, to hang his head and cry.
> —*I'm So Lonesome I Could Cry*

Now Slim, he's a testament to the peripatetic lifestyle. He's only in one place at a time, but he doesn't stay long once he gets there. He just keeps going. A testament because he's been at it for thirty-three years, since he got out of the service at twenty-one into the arms of a prosperous America, top of the world. Before Kennedy and before the Beatles and the hippies and Vietnam and Nixon with all the bullshit exploding around the country until the USA became a barely remembered dream, a laughable thing, emasculated, and useless as a cap blowing down Main Street. No, he emerged from compulsory service to his country at the tail end of the greatest nation on Earth with nearly every citizen still believing in it.

Well, Slim almost believed it. But something happened the day he left Sheppard Air Force Base, fully and honourably discharged with $118.63 in his pocket. A reborn civilian. A young man with his whole life lined up in front of him and feeling charmed. But that *but*—a moment that seemed like all the lights coming on at once in a dark room.

He'd stopped for a few goodbye-good-luck drinks with the boys in the enlisted men's club. Ketch and Springer, his two best buddies over the previous eighteen months, had bought him all the booze they thought he wanted. By early afternoon, Springer was snoring in his chair and Slim was beginning to worry about missing the bus into town.

"Kee-ryst on a stick, Slim," Ketch wailed and moved his arm to focus on his wristwatch, "don't get your pecker in a twist. That bus ain't leaving for a couple hours, anyway. Have another bourbon. This here might be the last time the three of us sit down together for a long time." As it turned out, it would be the absolute final occasion, but no one knew that then, not even Slim.

"I just don't want to spend any more time on-base than I have to, now that I'm a civilian," Slim explained again. He felt strangely sober, considering how much they'd been drinking and his companions' condition. He believed it had something to do with beginning the next stage of his life. He was excited at the prospect of joining his cousin in the frozen food business. Boyd had promised him a stake in his new company, Sportsman TV Dinners, a perfect career opportunity, it seemed to Slim. "You military types got to put up with it, but guys like me don't." He'd already changed into jeans, T-shirt and a nylon windbreaker.

"Balls," Ketch said, and tried to climb out of his chair to buy another round.

"Don't get up," Slim said. "I'll order for you." He picked up his duffle bag, patted his friend on the shoulder and, on his way out the door, tossed the bartender a deuce. "Bring them two guys a couple more drinks, and have one yourself."

He made the bus on time, rattling into Wichita Falls where the driver pulled into the Greyhound depot. By this time, the drinks had worked their way to his bladder, so the last few miles on the service vehicle, which had been built without the word "comfort" in the plans, had been physically painful to Slim. He hurried into the men's room behind a guy as big around as a pregnant mare. The large fellow stood at the sinks, looking down, resting his weight on his hands. As Slim felt the pleasure of release at the urinal, he became aware of the puffing and wheezing behind him.

Slim zipped up and turned to wash his hands just as the other man began to crumple to the floor. Without thinking about their relative sizes, Slim, who was appropriately named, tried to catch the falling colossus. Not a good idea. The two of them fell over together and Slim smacked the back of his head on the porcelain behind him.

They lay on the bathroom floor for quite a while before someone came in and found them. To all appearances, they were both unconscious. But Slim was far from asleep. As he stared into the smooth, bulging face of the man beside him, Slim had already taken a bend in the road that meant almost none of the future he had imagined would come to pass.

At that moment, a storm began to build in him. And in the midst of this commotion, Slim saw that he could see whatever he wanted about the large man; he was an open book named Geary Foreman, and he'd had a minor heart attack, from which he would likely recover. He was a tractor salesman, three months past his thirtieth birthday, married with two daughters. Slim also knew that this man, once a boy living on a farm in central Kansas, had had a black lab pup that he loved and which his father shot when it got sick with meningitis. That Geary hadn't yet forgiven him for that act when his father died of a heart attack ten days after the incident. And that he'd lived with an unresolved sense of guilt and bitterness ever since.

Slim was pitched over with this rush of knowing about a stranger. In the time that he and Geary Foreman were on the floor, Slim also noticed that only the past was clear, the future obscured.

Two ambulances arrived for the men. Foreman's condition was assessed as critical and he was hurried to St. Mary's Hospital to begin collecting on his Blue Cross plan. Slim was dazed, partly because of the blow and partly with the static and crackle of impressions from the people around him. It was like being in a large room ringed with doors blowing open randomly, and trying to shut them, all the while being hit with fragments from these people's lives, like shrapnel. The ambulance attendant with a dark birthmark on his face, sensitive and fearful of the rejection it might bring; the other, who had played triple-A baseball until he broke his ankle; a driver who was secretly a lover of other men, admiring the curve of the birthmarked attendant's back.

"I'm fine," Slim insisted. "I'll be okay if you can just give me a few minutes. Let me clear my head."

The ex-ballplayer said, "Well, sir, you've taken a mighty serious wallop to the back of your head. We'd better escort you to the hospital as a precaution, make sure you don't wind up on the DL." Slim looked into his face and saw a younger man, dressed in a team uniform with cap and glove.

"All right," Slim said, hoping to get some distance on this thing that had happened to him. He felt a spike of panic rise in him, imagining the rest of his life in mental chaos. Wondering if he was like a satellite drifting out of orbit, losing contact with reality, he asked, "You ever play pro ball?"

The man answered as if someone had just walked up to him and guessed his exact weight. "Yes, sir, I did. How'd you know?"

"I just thought you move like a shortstop; and what you said about the disabled list."

Later, on the way to the hospital, he saw that he could shut it off at will. By concentrating on the immediate box of events he was living through, he could ignore the other thoughts. It wasn't easy, but it was possible.

The doctor who examined him found nothing more serious than a lump and a small bruise on his skull's occipital bone. Although Slim knew that focussing on shutting out the mental flashes made him appear a bit disoriented, he insisted he was fine and would like to be on his way.

Slim walked back to the bus depot, but instead of going in and buying a ticket to Los Angeles, as he had planned, he just kept walking. He lugged his thoughts over the hills and valleys of what made up his life; he thought of who he was and where he might find his place. He walked a long while past the suburbs and out into the country where the road and a railway bridge crossed the Wichita River. The sun was setting and a light rain began to fall. Feeling that it was time to stop and plan where to go from there, he climbed down under the highway bridge.

In the dank gloom, he almost stepped on a dark-skinned man reclining against a shoulder pack. This fellow opened his eyes. "Welcome, friend. Have a seat; it's almost supper time."

His long, fine fingers held a bit of fishing line, which led out into the river. "Name's R. Dean Webster," he said, extending his hand.

Slim had tucked into himself so completely he didn't realize he'd been unaware of the world around him. The touch of R. Dean's hand set him off, but in a different manner from before. A tide of calm and clarity washed over Slim, and beyond all the details he suddenly knew about his new acquaintance, he understood that here was someone who had something he wanted.

After they had introduced themselves, R. Dean looked into Slim's face and asked, "So, just what exactly is it that's on your mind?"

Without waiting for an answer, he hauled in his line and Slim saw that about a dozen hooks branched off from it. Half of them had small, squirming crayfish attached, which R. Dean plucked off and dropped into a large can he had beside him. Some of the hooks without crayfish still had kernels of corn on them. R. Dean looked into the tin and said, "This should about do us."

"You know," R. Dean said, "some people feel a kinship with the ocean, and there's folks in Florida who swear they'd dry up and drop like dust without their swamp. But me, I like rivers. They're always coming from some place and going somewhere else. It don't make no difference to the river, though; it'll still be there the next time you look." He fished the now-pink crayfish from the boiling water and handed Slim some, piled on top of the corn he'd cooked in the same water. "Eat, young fella. There's a train to catch in thirty minutes."

R. Dean ran ahead of Slim, alongside the clunking, whining boxcar. "Don't worry," he'd said, "you'll know what to do when the time comes." He'd explained how to grab the handle on the door and swing into the open car, adding his body's inertia to the force of the moving train. He'd insisted the train would slow almost to a crawl before it crossed the rail bridge, but it still seemed to be moving pretty fast to Slim's way of thinking.

The funny thing was, R. Dean was right. The moment his fingers closed around the pitted metal handle, it was as if the train just kind of stopped and let Slim swing himself up and in. Beside him, R. Dean sat smiling in the dark. "I told you it'd be easy as opening your eyes in the morning."

Once over the bridge, the train began to pick up speed, moving through the night toward the unseen mountains in the west. R. Dean was soon asleep, curled up against his pack on the wooden floor. For a long while, Slim stared out into the dark and watched the moon weave in and out of the clouds. He eventually noticed that tears were rolling down his cheeks. Slim dug the heels of his thumbs into his face and wiped it dry.

3. Along the Way

> We don't get nearer or further or closer than a country mile . . .
> —*Why Don't You Love Me*

Broken clouds piled up above the surface of the Pacific, near the horizon, promising San Diego a cool evening in exchange for the afternoon heat. Zone watched the weather from the back of a Lincoln Continental, five storeys high in a Harbor

Drive parkade, eating take-out from the sushi bar at Basho's Frog.

"Man," said one of two colossal bikers wearing Gypsy Wheeler colours in the front seat, "I hate this raw fish crap. Why couldn't you get some fucking American food for a change?" He was called Tucker (from Friar Tuck, which he hated) because of his large, round body and because he'd spent part of his childhood in a Jesuit orphanage.

"You mean ground-up cow parts and processed potatoes, rendered in a sea of grease?" answered Ska, his ratty dreadlocks bouncing with righteousness, and a finger missing from his left hand, which waved a piece of cuttlefish. "That stuff will fill your heart with lard until the wrath of Jah whips your tubby ass out from under you."

"At least I'd die with a fucking smile on my face."

Zone was there to get the details of a delivery from these bikers, longshoremen who needed someone to take goods from point A to point B, no questions asked, all things bright and beautiful, and they paid well. This was his first such transaction and he chose to think of it as a service provided.

He'd met Ska and Tucker at the Nameless, where he served food and drinks. He'd noticed them a few times talking to Sherri Manyskies, the bar manager and a Lakota Indian with blue eyes and a waterfall of thick dark hair Zone longed to dive into. One evening, Sherri had called him over to their table. "Hey, Zone, these guys are curious about your tattoo," she said, pointing to the arrow and target only partly visible under the short sleeves of his black shirt. Zone pulled the sleeve up to his shoulder.

"Nice work," said the bulbous one, whose arms were detailed to the wrists like a furry copy of a Bosch painting. "Local?"

"No, I got it done in Mexico," he answered. "My cousin's friend."

They talked for a while about Mexico and tattoos, then

Zone got a call to the kitchen, and that was it until later when Sherri asked him if he wanted to make a thousand dollars on his weekend. She explained who they were and said she occasionally made deliveries for them around the city. "No guns or heavy drugs," she said. "Mostly just unusual items."

"What does that mean?"

"Maybe you'll see, if you do the job."

"Haven't they heard of UPS?"

Sherri looked at him for a moment, then smiled and said they needed something taken to Phoenix, and she didn't drive.

Zone left the parkade with the keys to a primer-grey Nissan truck they said he'd find the following afternoon, parked in the same spot the Lincoln had occupied. He also had a slip of paper with a Phoenix address and ten, worn fifties in his pocket. He'd enjoyed the feeling of being in a movie when Ska said he'd get another ten bills at the other end. The merchandise would be in a locked tool box in the back of the pickup.

Once Zone crossed the Colorado River into Arizona, he pretty well had the highway to himself—king of the road, except for a few gargantuan transport rigs. Driving through the night without sleep had awakened his mental funny bone, sending him a dust storm of minor hallucinations, like coyotes running beside him in the dark. Between Mohawk and Gila Bend, while searching for something to attend to besides asphalt and the lightening planes of the outstretched desert, he spotted a person walking along the shoulder.

At first he thought the figure was a road sign, but when he got closer, the sign became a man. He appeared to be floating just above the gritty surface of the shoulder. Zone slowed his truck and pulled up next to this lean but sturdy-looking character carrying a bulging, board-frame backpack. "Good morning," Zone shouted through the open window on the truck's passenger side, "can I give you a lift?"

"Well, son, that would be much appreciated." The man's whiskered face blossomed into a wide grin. He swung the pack into the rear of the pickup and climbed into its cab. Zone noticed his passenger's dusty cowboy boots, and realized the floating, too, had been illusion.

A country oldies station on the radio played Hank Williams singing, "Why don't you love me like you used to do?" The passenger, Perry, began to sing along, accomplishing what Zone thought was a passable imitation of Hank's voice.

"That's pretty good," Zone said.

"Thanks. I've had a lot of time on my hands to practise." Perry explained that he'd worked with Hank for a few shows in the early fifties. "And living in the desert, well, there's plenty of opportunity to entertain myself."

"How long have you been here?" Zone asked.

"About twenty years. Although, it sure don't feel like that long. Some days it seems that my life's all folded up like a highway map. It's only when I sit down and open it that I can see how far I've been." Perry pointed to a left-turn lane up ahead. "I guess you better let me off," he said. "I live a ways down this here road."

"It's no problem, I'll take you." Zone didn't mind going out of his way for this man. For some reason, he felt as if he'd met up with a close friend he'd been looking for, someone who truly understood his place in the world.

Perry lived next to a small arroyo, which he claimed wasn't on any map, so he'd named it Recuerdo Wash. "Most of the year that creek bed is dryer than the surface of the moon," he said. "But every spring there's water enough to lie down and bathe in." He nodded toward the middle one of three wooden buildings. "Come on in; I'll fix you some coffee and hotcakes before you go. A fella's got to eat breakfast."

Perry cooked on a two-burner gas hotplate set on top of a chipped white-enamel woodstove. Zone sipped his coffee and studied the inside of the one-room cabin. The furniture was simple, but the walls supported a matrix of rough shelves displaying various natural-world artifacts: tiny, bleached animal skulls; the sloughed skin of a rattlesnake; most of a grey-papery wasp nest; a row of fossilized seashells embedded in stone; the dusty dried husk of a spider the size of a child's glove . . .

"You ever spend time in the desert?" Perry asked.

"Only passing through," Zone said. "Like today." And then he suddenly remembered. "Except once," he said. "My dad took me camping near my uncle's place in La Esperanza before he died. I must have been about three. Yeah—I haven't thought about that for years; it seems like something from another life."

"Ain't it funny the things that'll hide in a person's mind and then come out and reveal themselves when the time is right?" Perry said as he set two plates of food on the table and sat down to eat.

Later, they walked down across Recuerdo Wash, then up a small rise which provided a view of the desert and Castle Dome peak in the north. Perry pointed out a dun-coloured bird perched beside an oval nest on a spiny cholla branch. "Cactus wren," he said. "Them birds build three or four nests each season, but they only lay eggs in one. The others are just shelters." In the distance, clouds had begun to gather along the tops of the mountains. Zone looked at his watch and said, "I guess I better get rolling. I want to be in Phoenix today, then San Diego again by tomorrow afternoon for my shift at the restaurant."

"What are you doing, driving all that way and back on a weekend—winning a bet?"

"Working. Sort of." Zone told Perry about the bikers and the delivery of whatever was in the back of the truck.

"Aren't you curious what you're hauling?" Perry asked.

It turned out that Perry knew a bit about picking locks, and figured he could open the box—which ran across the width of the pickup's bed—without damaging it. "If you walk enough roads, you learn a lot of tricks," he said, his concentration on working a length of wire into the mouth of the lock. Zone watched the older man's long fingers, gritty and callused, cradling the heavy padlock as he tugged, then slid its shackle out of the hasp on the box lid.

Inside, among assorted tools, ropes and cable, was a metal container, about the size of a large tackle box, with chromed fasteners. This was stuffed with styrofoam beads protecting what appeared to be three ancient Mayan artifacts: a greening bronze knife, crescent blade topped with a stout, broad-faced figure, his headdress set with chips of abalone shell; a terra cotta bowl, incised with Mayan hieroglyphs; and a stylized, feathered serpent, fashioned from silver and turquoise.

"Quetzalcoatl," Perry said, hefting the silver figure, which coiled in toward a wide face frozen in a toothy grimace. "The god of wisdom and self-sacrifice."

None of the pieces was larger than the length of Zone's hand. He realized the only surprise he felt at the discovery of these items was that he wasn't surprised. They were somehow half-familiar, like things often seen but never really looked at before.

"Well, sir," Perry said, placing the Quetzalcoatl image

carefully back into the box, "my guess is these are pretty much genuine."

As he drove from Perry's to Phoenix, Zone tried to pin down the source of familiarity his cargo held for him. A few times, he felt he almost had his hands on it, then it slipped away, elusive. But he was pleasantly agitated, a bit in awe of the three small artifacts. He travelled that highway as if he were moving through the heart of another sort of treasure. The crisp blue above and the landscape surrounding him illuminated by a light that seemed to cast no shadows.

By early afternoon he had reached Phoenix, and he stopped at a gas station to buy a map. A teenage girl in a booth walled around with bullet-proof Plexiglas took his money and passed him a city guide on a tray which moved under the glass. The ring on her index finger was silver with a turquoise turtle. Zone found his destination on the map, then asked her the best way to get there. "I don't really know," the girl said. "I'm not from around here."

He laughed. "I know what you mean. Well, can you show me where I am right now?" He slid the map back to her and watched as she marked a small X in one corner.

Zone returned to the truck and traced out, on the grid of streets and avenues, what looked like a good route to follow. He placed the map on the seat beside him, then pulled out into traffic. He knew he'd have to stop thinking about the metal box locked away in back, and concentrate on getting it home.

Constraints of Gravity

The early-hour blues had not taken hold, but he felt them approaching. Another Sunday morning, last day of the weekend, the long, yellow-papery light of late afternoon hours away, but already on Rudi's mind. He drank instant because he was impatient, although it tasted like a mere suggestion of coffee, lacking the sense-sharpening resins of the real thing.

His face felt buttered, his hair still twisted from sleep. On the radio, tuned to an oldies easy-listening station, Dean Martin slurred, "You're nobody, till somebody loves you." How would he know? Frank Sinatra's flagman, a career built on pretending to be drunk and hanging around with Mafia royalty. Rudi was ready to vent grievance, to find fault and unearth bitter nuggets from the potato field of his mind.

He stirred his second cup, the action lost in a scrap of memory—Nescafé jars on restaurant tables in Mexico twenty years earlier. He'd visited there between two week-long engagements at hotel lounges in San Diego. That was when he was still trying, still pushing his life along. Even in high school he'd realized he would have to work hard to rise above being ordinary. Music had been Rudi's chosen elevator, but he never seemed to get past about the third floor.

When the phone rang, the intrusion was startling, his response a shot of adrenaline more potent than anything the coffee had so far delivered. Rudi's hand jerked and spilled some of the liquid onto the counter. Christ almighty, he thought. Who could be calling him? He grabbed the dishcloth out of the sink and set it under his cup before answering. "What?" he demanded.

Rudi listened a moment to silence, then, at the point of hanging up, heard a deep voice. "Let me speak to Carlene," it said.

"Wrong number," Rudi answered.

"Bullshit. I know she's there. Put her on." The voice had a more realistic touch of alcohol damage than the Dean Martin song, just then winding into its orchestral exit.

"There's no one here named Carlene. In fact, no one's here but me, and I bet even you can tell I'm not Carlene." Rudi dropped the receiver into its cradle.

He was wiping up the spilled coffee when the phone rang again. This time, he didn't jump. "Hello," he said.

"Let me speak to Carlene." The same voice, the same malt-thick tone.

"Listen, this is a wrong number. There's no Carlene here. I don't even know anyone named Carlene."

"Just put her on. I've got a right to talk to her."

"This has nothing to do with rights," Rudi said. "Pay attention: she's not here; don't call this number again."

The next time the phone rang, he was eating toast and

reading the community newspaper's column on local crime—how the incidence of violent attacks was rising.

"Don't hang up on me again, asshole, or I'll come over there and drag her out in the street and kick your butt around the block while I'm at it." The voice sounded clearer, less rippled.

Rudi wondered what this guy had been doing in the half-hour that had passed, and why he had called again. "Why are you harassing me?" he asked. "I told you I don't know anyone named Carlene."

"You know her, all right. I'm not stupid. You think I haven't seen you putting moves on her between sets, playing special songs for her on that fucking organ? She's always been a sucker for a serenade."

For a moment Rudi couldn't speak. The voice on his phone had suddenly passed from the realm of annoyance to that of potential danger. The caller knew something about him that made Rudi doubt it was a wrong number. But even this knowledge was twisted.

"It was an electric piano, but I don't play any more," Rudi said. "I haven't had a gig for three years. You've got me mixed up with someone else."

"You're the one who's mixed up, you piss-whistling lounge reptile, and you're going to pay for it. Now, hand the phone to Carlene—"

Rudi heard a woman shouting in the background, the sound abruptly muffled by a hand or some other object placed over the mouthpiece. He waited, twisting the tie of his faded, blue tartan bathrobe around his finger, and then the caller hung up.

The next day, on his shift at the 7-Eleven, Rudi was preoccupied with the telephone business of the previous morning. He handed a regular customer king-size though she always asked for menthol, and later confused a mix of lottery tickets. An intense-looking man, tall, thin with shaved head and a single earring, who came into the store frequently, shouted at him when he overcharged for an *Easy Rider* magazine and a medium root beer Slurpee.

"Hey, goofus," the man said, looking from his change to his magazine and drink, "this isn't fucking right."

Rudi apologized and corrected his mistake, but the man left the store muttering, and gave the glass door a rattling kick on the way out.

Rudi was relieved when Winnie, the Chinese woman who only worked mornings, went home at noon and Dannae took over from her. Dannae was taller than Rudi, with close-cropped blonde hair and skin that stayed tanned all year. She always arrived on her skateboard, even on rainy days, and Rudi had long since gotten over his feelings of intimidation around her. He liked working with her, if for no other reason than that the school kids who came in to play *Mortal Kombat* and steal chocolate bars were afraid of her. Him they just called Barney, presumably because the maroon-coloured jackets the district manager insisted they wear reminded them of the children's TV dinosaur. "Hey, Barney," one of them had hollered when he chased them out for knocking over a rack of potato chips, "what about the happy fucking family?" They never dared to call Dannae names.

"So, Rudi," Dannae said, "how was your weekend?"

"Don't ask," he answered, but he was anxious to tell someone about the phone calls. Before she got to the back office, he began to uncoil his account of the events that had wound themselves so completely around him.

"That's totally bizarre," she said. "Did you get the jerk's number?"

"How would I do that?"

Dannae explained how to use the phone to get a caller's number, and Rudi marvelled at the younger generation's knowledge of technology.
"What technology?" she said. "It's only the telephone."

Rudi was almost afraid to go home when his shift ended, and hung around talking to Dannae until he could sense she was bored with his complaints and concerns. He didn't feel up to cooking, so he walked to the drive-through window of an A&W near his apartment, and bought a hamburger. Then he spent the rest of the evening in front of the TV, imagining dialogue between himself and mister Carlene. About 3:30, he woke to the sight of John Carradine dying in Joan Crawford's arms, and a voice assuring him the exciting conclusion to *Johnny Guitar* would follow the break.

It was Thursday midnight when the next call came, and by then Rudi had begun to file the incident away as one of the mysteries of modern life. When he answered, he could hear the chaotic soundscape of a busy tavern in the background. "Carlene," the voice, raspy as smoked eel, insisted. "Let me speak to Carlene."

Rudi hung up immediately, dialled star-69 and copied down the number on the back of a Pizza Hut menu he kept on the kitchen counter. He wasn't surprised when it turned out he'd been called from a pay phone. But he wished he'd spoken to the guy, used some of the great lines he'd been concocting for just that moment.

"It must have been the moon or something," Dannae said when he told her about the latest phone call. "And we're out of pepperoni sticks."

"What do you mean?" Rudi asked.

"About the moon or the sausage?"

"The moon. I know how to deal with pepperoni." Rudi took a notebook out from beneath the cash register and added the item to the manager's order list.

"Last night I saw that skinhead," she said. "The one who's always in here buying biker mags and Slurpees?"

"He's a skinhead?"

Dannae looked at Rudi, smiled and rolled her eyes. "Anyway, he got his nose busted for arguing with an off-duty firefighter in the Waldorf lounge."

"That guy's a real skinhead?"

She held two fingers on her upper lip and gave a straight-arm salute. "Sieg Heil," she said.

"What time was that?" Rudi asked.

"Fairly early—I was gone long before last call."

"Well," Rudi said, "mister Carlene didn't sound like he had a broken nose."

Early Sunday afternoon, Rudi returned home from Safeway with three plastic bags of groceries. As he put his key in the lock, his phone began ringing. He pushed the door open, dropped the bags on the hall floor and ran across the living-room carpet without taking off his shoes. This time he was ready. "Hello," he barked.

The voice seemed to be coming from under water. "Put Carlene on," it gurgled, "now."

"Listen, mister Carlene," Rudi said, "concentrate your tiny brain on the following message: there's no one named Carlene here, or anywhere near this place." Rudi's eyes shone; a drop of sweat rolled down the inside of his armpit.

"That's it, man," the voice said, "I'm through with warning you."

"And I'm through listening to your line of crap," Rudi answered. "Why don't you come over?" He opened a drawer and saw the lightweight tack hammer he kept there. "I've got a hefty little ball-peen I'd like to bounce off your thick skull."

"You're dead, pal. Good as," mister Carlene answered and then hung up.

Once Rudi had the number, he changed his clothes and put his groceries away. He sat in the kitchen, holding the piece of paper on which he'd scrawled the seven digits, an east-end exchange, like his. He watched a gull the size of a cocker spaniel chase three pigeons from a choice perch on the cornice of the building across the alley. By dinner time, no one had come pounding on his door, and his telephone had remained as silent as a toaster.

Finally, he lifted the receiver and dialled. He felt weightless, outside the constraints of gravity. He was surprised when a woman answered, but he cleared his throat and spoke. He stuttered out an explanation, that there'd been several calls, including one a few hours earlier. He said they'd come from this number and he would like to speak to the man of the house.

The woman laughed and said, "There's no man here. You've got a wrong number."

Rudi dialled the number again. "Are you sure there's no man? He called from your phone."

"Stop bothering me," she said. "I already told you. Leave me alone or I'll call the cops."

After that, Rudi didn't have much appetite. He ate tuna from the can with a slice of bread and a beer, and lay on the couch with the lights off. He fell asleep and dreamed he was a boy. His father wanted to look at his homework, but he couldn't remember where it was or if he'd really done it.

Finally, the ringing phone woke him, propelling him out of his nightmare into the now dark room. He smiled as he moved to answer the phone, and in his mind began to sing along with Dean Martin.

They Almost Quench Your Thirst

Today I walked the whole way from Keremeos to Osoyoos. I got tired of holding my thumb out, trying to look all right, a safe bet for anyone with a little kindness in their heart. Hell with them. No one even slowed down, so after an hour or maybe more, I started walking past the fruit stands into that dry, hot landscape, while transport rigs and RVs with bicycles strapped on the back roared past, whipping sand up into my eyes. Wind almost shoving me to the dirt. A bunch of cows stood beside an old broken-down shed and stared at me. I threw a rock at them, hit one right in the face and it hardly flinched. I threw another, but missed and shouted at the cows: "Go fuck yourselves, goddamn worthless beasts," and kept walking.

The sun was baking me, so I took my extra shirt out of the pack and tied it over my head. Must've looked like an Arab. Lawrence of the Okanagan. Below the highway, in the Kettle River valley, are fields of vegetables and orchards so green they almost quench your thirst just looking at them. What would it be like to live there? I wondered. I wished I had an apple as red and juicy as the one painted on the sign that was nothing but that apple and an arrow pointing toward those green fields. "Fruit and veg" it said under the arrow. I threw a rock at the sign, too.

Over and over I filled my lungs with the sweet sage air, filled my head with it so I wouldn't think of anything else. My heavy boots followed each other along the shoulder of the road, dusty, remote. I wanted to keep my mind in the present, but when I saw the sign for the turnoff to the Night Hawk border-crossing, I suddenly pictured you sitting on the bed in that shitty little room above the Avalon.

What did you think when you woke up and realized I was gone? Did you make the bed, as usual? Go down to the café, buy a pack of Rothman's from J-J and ask casually, while lighting your first smoke of the day, if I'd come in yet?

Just before the highway begins its last long downhill into Osoyoos, there's a patch of what look like salt pools, crusty white and filled with green-blue water. I remember when we passed them on the bus to the coast you said, "How can something be so ugly and so beautiful at the same time?" I laughed then because I wasn't sure if you really wanted an answer. Now, I'm not certain I know what you meant by the question, or whether you were even talking about the pools. All I know is, tomorrow I'm sticking my thumb out—I'm never going to walk that far again, not if I can help it.

Wrapped in Blue

He was sitting at the bottom of a swimming pool, all the world around him the tropical-water blue of painted pool walls. His body was young again and strong, and he was pleased to discover he could breathe under water, as long as he kept still. Thea was there, too, swimming in front of him, pointing at her wristwatch and then at the surface as if to say it was time to go. Her hair gathered in two ponytails at the sides, the way she'd looked as a twelve-year-old, before Cynthia died.

Clive opened his eyes into a room tinted by the turquoise numbers on his alarm clock. Four-thirty. Too early to get up, but he knew he wouldn't get back to sleep, would simply toss around until he became more sick of being in bed than he dreaded getting out of it.

Passing through the kitchen, he turned on the coffee maker, which he had prepared the night before, then showered and dressed for work. He checked inside his nostrils in the mirror for the dark hairs which seemed to grow faster than the hair on his head. His hand fluttered slightly, holding the silver folding scissors as he carefully snipped and trimmed. He thought about the dream, the feeling of being wrapped in blue. The colour of Aqua Velva. He'd once seen a couple in a Gastown alley sharing a bottle of the aftershave. At least I never got that low, he thought. "Not that desperate," he said, and hearing the scratch in his voice, cleared his throat.

After breakfast, he sat at the big Hammond organ in the living room. The only photos he kept in frames rested on its flat top—one of Cynthia, holding the newborn Thea, and the other of the three of them the last summer they'd vacationed at the lake. The elaborate keyboard stood out like an altar in his small house with its otherwise plain furniture. Cynthia had yearned for a Hammond, but they'd always needed a dozen other things more. He bought it two years after she died, shortly before Thea left. The thing cost a fortune, but the price included a year's worth of free lessons. He could still only play a few melodies with his right hand, following the instrument's canned accompaniment. All day, all night Mary Anne—*Boom chicka, boom chicka*; down by the seashore, sifting sand—*Boom chicka, boom chicka.*

He wondered if his dream meant Thea might call. He often tried to imagine her life in Winnipeg with Cynthia's sister. Thea had told him she felt too alone with him, and asked to move to her Aunt Lorene's, at least to finish high school. She got a job there, weekends and some evenings at a Husky station west of the city, and wrote that she was saving money. The last time he'd phoned—at Thanksgiving—she'd brought up her plan to go to university in that prairie city. He guessed he should feel proud about that, at least, and told her he was. But mostly he missed having her in his life.

Clive left the house earlier than usual for the learning centre where he taught adults to read and write. His work day technically began at 10, but he was generally there by 9 to have more than the allotted hour for one-on-one work in the open area. He hated the way individual contact with students had been sacrificed to accommodate large-group classes simply because they brought the district more education dollars from the province.

The parking lot was almost empty when he arrived. Rob Redhead, his principal, was paying a cab driver and made a show of looking at his watch when he spotted Clive. "Did you piss your bed?" He laughed. "Or are you trying to impress the administration?"

Clive smiled. "Where's your car today?" he asked.

"Had to take it to the dealer's for a warranty check. Jennie needed the van, so I'm cabbing it. I don't suppose you could give an old pal a ride home after work?" Clive and Rob had once been friends, back in the days when they were both new to teaching—when Clive still drank and before Rob had become a principal.

"No problem," Clive said. He had to force a friendly look onto his face. He felt as if Rob had changed sides at some point, and occasionally had to make excuses not to spend time with him. Also, Rob's drinking was hard for Clive to be around. Even after two years, he was sometimes tempted to fall back on old habits. On the days when he felt most empty, he went home and sat at the Hammond, drinking coffee instead of vodka and pecking away at melodies like "Yellow Bird"—ones that wouldn't feed his dark mood. *Up high in banana tree. Boom chicka, boom chicka.*

In the school, a half-dozen students sat scattered around the tables. He waved at two Punjabi women who smiled and waved back as they kept up an intense, rapid conversation. Brad, an unemployed welder, hunkered down in his regular place beneath the clock, reading an abridged and simplified version of *Great Expectations*. Clive noticed that Brad still moved his blunt fingers along the text as if he were trying to push the words into meaning.

"How's the book?" Clive asked.

"Not too bad," Brad answered. "Better than watching wrestling." This was a private joke they shared from Brad's first day at the centre.

"Good game last night. But that was a cheap shot Chelios took at Joe."

Another secret they shared was that Brad's cousin played NHL hockey. Not a star, but well-enough known that Brad could have gained a certain kind of status at the centre if he'd let others in on it. Clive wasn't sure whether humility or insecurity kept him quiet. "You want to work on reading today?"

Brad tucked a paper match into the book to mark his place and opened his vinyl briefcase. "Actually, I need some help filling these out." He put several forms on the table; the top one had a familiar government logo.

Clive asked, "Passport application?" He had helped dozens of students with these.

"I'm applying for a job in Saudi," Brad said. "Here …" He dug around in the valise until he found a wrinkled piece of newspaper, which he handed to Clive. "Melanie's mom saw this in the paper. Thought I should give it a shot." Brad hadn't had a job for a year and a half, since he'd fallen from a catwalk inside a ship he was working on. The fall had hurt his back so badly he hadn't been able to get out of bed for two months. "They're building a pulp mill in the desert," he said. "Gonna make sandpaper." He laughed, but watched carefully for Clive's response. "It's refinery work. I did that for three years in Alberta, so I should be a ringer."

Clive smiled at Brad, then returned the clipping and picked up the top sheet from the stack. "Well, Mr. Ringer," he said, "let's take a stab at this."

After lunch, Rob called Clive into his office. "Have a seat," he said, and closed the door. He opened his bottom filing cabinet door, and took out a mickey of J&B Scotch. He pulled two small paper cups from his water cooler and began pouring.

"Not for me, thanks," Clive said.

Rob held the open bottle in one hand, the cap in the other. Sunlight through the window gleamed off the green glass, full of promises. "Still on the wagon?"

Clive leaned forward in his chair. "What's up? I've got a writing class at one."

Rob screwed the top back on the bottle and put it away. "Hannington was in yesterday." Clive had seen the superintendent sniffing around the centre, pretending to make jovial conversation with students, but Clive suspected he was really counting heads, tallying the government money. "He wants larger classes; says it's necessary to move away as much as possible from the one-on-one. Says the Ministry would flip out if they knew how much inefficiency they're funding."

"Coming from him, that's real irony."

Rob looked at Clive, eyes wide in mock surprise. "Are you suggesting—"

"Nothing would make those guys happier," Clive said, "than to get the green light to run this place like a cattle ranch. What did you tell him?"

"I said I'd have to talk it over with my staff. Get some impressions from the front line."

Maybe he hasn't sold out completely, Clive thought. "Well, you can tell him my front line impression is that efficiency doesn't always equal effectiveness."

"Clive, I'm doing my best. It's just a matter of time. Once the board makes its mind up ..." Rob raised his hand in a gesture of helplessness.

Clive stood. "You should talk to the rest of the staff about this," he said, "but I don't think you'll find much disagreement."

"Are we still on for three?" Rob asked.

For a moment, Clive felt something like fear punch through him. Then he remembered his promise of a ride. "Sure. Of course. I'll come and get you."

As Clive turned out of the parking lot, Rob asked him if he'd mind stopping at the Princeton, a pub down near the docks and on the way to Rob's house. "You don't have to come in," he said. "I just want to pick up some beer."

Clive wasn't happy about getting that close to a place where he'd once had a seat at the regulars' table. But he took the familiar turn off Grandview and headed north toward the water.

Rob was in a jolly mood. He wanted to talk about the old days, people they'd known and wild times they'd shared. Clive could smell the whiskey on him, a trace of the alcohol that was slowly etching a garden of rum blossoms across his cheeks. Rob had the window down so he could smoke; even so, the sharp tang of burning tobacco drifted around inside the car and stung Clive's eyes.

"Hey," Rob said. "I bumped into Rossiter last week. Thought he'd be dead by now." They were stopped at a light and Rob flicked the butt of his cigarette onto the sidewalk. "He's limping worse than ever, but he's lucky to still be walking around."

"Yeah, he's a very fortunate human being, all right," Clive said. He regretted the self-righteous edge that now came into his speech whenever he spent time in Rob's presence, and spoke quickly to try to counter it. "That night he broke his leg, Christ, I thought he was going to die. All that mud and him vomiting." It had been raining for days, and a bunch of them had left the Princeton to go to Point Roberts. They'd been arguing about great wrestlers and Gene Kiniski's name came up. Rossiter said Kiniski owned a pub across the border, and with the logic of drunks, they decided to make the trip. Rossiter drove and somewhere in Richmond they went off the road. When he got out to see what was wrong, he slipped and fell down the embankment. Clive heard him scream, got out of the car, too, and slid down the slope on his ass; he could still remember pulling up Rossiter's pant leg and being surprised by the bone poking out of the skin. "I don't think I'll ever forget that night."

Rob laughed. "Neither will Rossiter."

Clive remembered Cynthia waiting up on the couch when he got home. He realized that in all the excitement, he'd forgotten to call to let her know where he was. She looked so grim, huddled into her blue terry cloth bathrobe. Defensiveness and anger leapt through him. He expected her to say something about the mud now dried and caked on his hair and clothing.

"We have to talk, Clive," she'd said. "I saw Dr. Hart today." And he'd felt quickly deflated, remembering that she had been scheduled to get her test results, and knew from her tone that what she had to say would not be good news.

Clive crossed the intersection and swung into the lot behind the pub. "I'll wait here," he said, and shut off the engine. Two men and a woman sat on one of the concrete dividers near the entrance to the pub. They looked like last year's fruit, left hanging on the tree all winter.

Rob got out, shut the door, then bent his face down to the open window. "Back in a sec," he said, and winked.

He'd been waiting about ten minutes, wondering what the hold-up could be, when one of the men approached his car. His clothes looked like they'd been used as rags in a garage. "Hey pal," the man said, "could you help us out with some bus fare?" He pointed back at the others, who watched impassively from their perch. "My wife needs to get to her doctor's appointment."

Clive looked at him, noticed both his top front teeth were chipped. "I'll give you two bucks if you go into the bar and see if my friend's there," he said.

"Well, jeez, you know, they just threw us out. I can't go back in or they'll call the cops. Is there something else I can do?"

Clive dug in his pocket and handed the man two dollars. "Never mind," he said. He got out of the car and locked it.

He was amazed how little the place had changed in two years. The same antique prints of ships and locomotives hung around the walls. Even the haze of smoke that clouded the room seemed the same. He didn't recognize the bartender but some of the faces around the room were familiar. A woman named Louise came past with a tray of empties, glanced at him and did a double take. "Hello, stranger," she said. "Didn't expect to see you around here again." Her teeth were different: whiter, straighter. "What can I do you for?"

"I'm just looking for Rob Redhead; no drinks for me, thanks." Clive tried to appear friendly, casual, but he felt again the fear that had touched him in Rob's office. Louise directed him to the far corner, near the window. There, he was surprised to see Rob sitting at a table with Brad, leaning forward in conversation and gesturing. There were two pints of beer on the table, and on the seat beside Rob, two paper bags from the bar's off-sales. Brad looked up with a grin when he saw Clive, and Rob turned around.

"There he is," Rob shouted. "Our man with the helping hand."

"Mr. Redhead says this place used to be your second home," Brad said.

"Mr. Redhead was supposed to buy his beer and come right back to the car," Clive said.

"Don't get all worked up, Clive." Rob pointed across the table. "And don't be rude to Brad. Have a seat and we'll go in a minute. We were just discussing the learning centre."

"I can wait in the car."

"Sit down. We'll take care of you, right, Brad?"

Clive pulled a chair over from the next table. The action felt strangely satisfying, like threading a bolt into place. "Finish up your beer and let's go," he said. He waved off a waiter headed in his direction.

"Brad believes the group classes are worthless," Rob said, "and I'm giving him the pedagogical rationale for them."

"What's that mean?" Brad said. "And I didn't say 'worthless,' just that I think working one-on-one with a teacher is the best way for a guy like me to learn."

"A guy like you?" Rob said. "But Brad, there are a lot of other students in the school who have different needs. Are you saying they're not important?"

Clive noticed that Brad's eyes had narrowed. He knew the young man didn't like to be spoken to as if he were a simpleton. "Don't listen to his bullshit," Clive said. "He's just jerking your chain." He remembered seeing Brad leave the school at noon and wondered how long he'd been in the pub before they got there.

"Well, fellas," Rob said. "Let's not forget that I am in charge of the place." He smirked and held his arms wide open as if he'd scored some great dialectical point.

"That doesn't make you any better than me, or anyone else in here." Brad's expression darkened. "In fact, there's plenty here who are ten times the man you are."

Rob looked around the room. He'd probably had arguments of this nature with half a dozen of the people there. "These losers?" he said, laughing.

Brad stood quickly, and bumped the table, spilling beer over the sides of the glasses. "Hey, hey," Rob said. "Clive was right, I'm just jerking your chain. These are fine men. You're a fine man. And this is fine beer. Let's drink it before it ends up on the floor."

Brad sat back in his chair, and picked up his pint. Rob clinked his glass against Brad's. "Cheers," he said, and drank to the bottom of the glass. Brad nodded curtly and took a sip. Clive wondered if he'd ever see Brad in the school again.

Clive didn't want to talk to Rob any more, so he drove and tried to stay outside the man's chatter. "I know a lot of people don't like me," Rob said. Clive looked over at him—Rob was fidgeting with the air vent in front of him on the dash. "It was different before I moved up. I had real friends once." He complained about his job and about Jennie's inability to understand the stresses it put on him. How he needed a drink now and then to keep his sanity.

"You don't know how lucky you are sometimes," Rob said. "No one nagging you, no kids making demands. You're on easy street and you don't appreciate it."

Clive swung the car violently to the right, down an alley, and stopped. He grabbed the lapel of Rob's blazer. "Don't you fucking dare," he said. "Don't say a thing about Cynthia or Thea or my life. For once, keep your goddamn mouth shut." He let go of the jacket, took a deep breath and stared out the front of the car. "In fact, it would be best if you stayed quiet until we get to your house."

They drove in silence the rest of the way. When Rob got out he thanked Clive as if nothing had happened and walked up the driveway to his door. It wasn't until two blocks later Clive realized Rob had had only one bag in his hands. He leaned over and felt under the passenger seat. He touched the paper and pulled the bag out. Inside were six cans of Lucky Lager.

Clive left the package on the floor and turned east, away

from his house. It began to rain and fat drops puckered on the windshield. He took Hastings to the Barnett Highway and headed out toward the beach at Belcarra. He and Cynthia had often driven out there when they were first dating. He wasn't sure what he'd do when he got there, but he knew he didn't want to go home yet, to spend the evening sitting at the Hammond. Fly me to the moon, *chicka boom, chicka.*

He drove mechanically, caught up in memories of the beach, of swimming out past the end of the pier. He was thinking about the dream he'd had that morning, how bright and lovely Thea had looked, when the streetlights lining the road blinked once and went out, along with all the other lights in the neighbourhood. The traffic signals weren't working either, so each intersection he came to was backed up with drivers trying to work out a stop-and-go order.

Finally, he parked his car and took the flashlight from the glove compartment. He flicked it on once to see that it still worked, then got out and opened the trunk. From an emergency kit he'd put together years before, he dug out a yellow rubberized poncho. The rain gear had been folded up for so long, he had to peel it apart in places. He put it on and walked back to the busy crossing he'd just gone through.

Carefully, he made his way out to the centre of the traffic. He stood there, using the flashlight and the hand signals he'd seen construction-site flaggers use hundreds of times. Within minutes, cars were flowing smoothly through the intersection. Some people beeped and waved as they passed. Clive smiled back and motioned them through. His feet were quickly soaked, but he didn't mind. In the middle of the rain and the confusion, he felt right at home.

Glass Houses

Gina told Kevin that when she was twelve her hobby was shoplifting make-up. Lying in bed one Sunday morning, she described how she and her friends would swarm into Woolworth's or Rexall Drugs and hang around, giggling and screeching over the Preparation H instructions or howling about the fun they could have with a few packages of Ex-Lax. They drew so much attention to themselves, no one suspected they were stealing. After a while, they'd buy a few bags of salt-and-vinegar shoestrings or a large bottle of cream soda, and leave. Behind the store, Gina, the queen bee, divided the take among them. Maybelline mascara, Revlon nail polish and a broad palette of lipstick shades. She had more eyeliner pencils than crayons.

These days, she cleans houses for other people, like Mrs. Miles, who inherited a bundle from her husband—the founder of the Miles Coffee Shop chain ("If you've got miles to go, get some Miles to go!"). Gina's stepfather had always bought two large styrofoam cups of their house blend at the start of every long, family car trip. "Fuel for the car; fuel for me," he said, winking at her in the back seat, while her mother laughed. The slightly burnt fragrance of the coffee mixed forever in her mind now with the yellow-toothed stench of his breath.

What surprises Gina most about the people she works for is some of the stuff they buy. Things she'd never waste a penny on, even if she had the inexhaustible fortune she imagines they possess. "That Mrs. Miles," she told Kevin, "she's nuts about glass. She's got a room full of crystal and glass ornaments. Candle holders, vases, butterflies, mermaids—one plate about this big," she said, holding her hands shoulder-width apart, "black with gold flecks inside the glass. I saw the price tag on the bottom of it. Five hundred dollars." Kevin shook his head and took the cigarette she had been holding in her left hand. They had just made love and she felt delicately carved, every facet of her body reflecting light.

"Too much money," he proclaimed, smoke drifting from his mouth and nose as he spoke. "Makes them lose perspective."

That was before Kevin disappeared, and she remembers feeling charmed, unbeatable, during their time together. Didn't leave a letter or any explanation. She wants to hold onto the feelings the memories give her, but doesn't trust them anymore.

When she gets home from work, Gina takes the pewter and glass angel from her purse and sets it on her room's single shelf. Each time a bus passes on the street below, the tiny figure trembles and moves closer to the edge. If it drops, thinks Gina, it'll smash into angel dust or a billion glittering slivers, each one waiting to pierce my skin, make me bleed. She imagines this, but she doesn't move toward the angel or try to catch it when it falls.

Chicken Man

In a chair beneath the ersatz starlit sky of the Waldorf Hotel's Polynesian lounge, Connor suddenly had a lucid moment. He knew what he needed to make his life right again. The only solution he could imagine to the huge knot of anger and poorly thought-out decisions he had become was to make a big change, and the most obvious leap into metamorphosis was to move far away from Vancouver. Because he'd lived all his life in the Lower Mainland of BC, the only people he knew well who didn't live in the city—Pete and Cheryl—had moved halfway across the province to the town of Nelson. Pete was an old friend, someone whose style and attitude Connor admired. But he wasn't sure if these were the right people to hook up with, since Pete was a cousin of the guy who'd run off with his wife and got him started on this unhappy path in the first place. Still, he believed he had few choices, and dialled the long-distance call from a pay phone in the hotel entrance.

Speakers mounted above the phone pounded out a country-rock tune, making it hard to hear what Pete was saying, but he seemed happy to hear from Connor.

"What's that?" Connor asked.

"I said, sure man, come on out to God's country," Pete answered. "The old lady will be glad to have some company, and with the baby and everything, we could use the extra money."

Connor appreciated that Pete didn't mention his cousin. Pete never dug into anyone else's business, and expected the same from others.

A few weeks later, Connor drove east in his old GM van that didn't have a working heater. This hadn't been a big problem on the coast, but the time of year was early spring and once he got to the Okanagan, snow was falling. He put on a toque and a pair of leather work gloves he kept in the tool box. Then he wrapped a blanket over his lap. Twice he had to stop to wipe down the inside of the windshield with anti-freeze to keep it clear. At first the drive felt like the beginning of an adventure, new opportunity opening for him. But eventually, his thoughts began to focus on the sorry state of his existence and he decided the broken heater was a perfect, and fitting, metaphor.

Outside Greenwood, he picked up a hitchhiker, a Native guy named Frank, who had no luggage and wore only work boots, jeans, a shirt and a denim jacket. Seeing him dressed like that, Connor guessed Frank must have thought him funny so he explained about the broken heater. "I've got another blanket in the back if you want," Connor said. "So you don't freeze your ass off."

"No. That's okay," Frank answered.

The next time Connor asked, Frank told him Indians don't feel the cold. "Lucky," Connor said.

Frank looked at him a moment as if trying to decide exactly what Connor meant. "Never thought of it that way," he said.

As he drove through a long, dark stretch of tamarack, spruce and small, weedy-looking lakes, Connor talked to Frank about how he was moving out of the city for the first time, how he was aiming for transformation. "In a big way, you know? I believe this might be the start of a whole new set of luck for me. They say you need to experience some adversity, some suffering and pain to really achieve major things."

Frank laughed. "If that was all it took, the Indian people would be the kings and queens of this country."

He didn't speak much, but even so, his presence softened both the way Connor had been feeling and the gloom of that drive from Greenwood to Grand Forks. Frank got out in front of the Winnipeg Hotel, and Connor wondered how it had got its name, so far from Manitoba. The sky had grown dark and snow had begun to fall again, though only lightly. Frank climbed out of the van and shouted, "Stay warm, buddy, and good luck," then walked on down the sidewalk, snowflakes drifting onto his jacket. Connor felt a bit strange, as if he should have been the one wishing Frank better fortune.

Just before Nelson, Connor crossed a bridge and turned onto a road that led him to an intersection where the pilings remained from an older bridge. From there he followed Frewer Road and counted the driveways, as Pete had described, until he came to the twelfth one. He parked at the roadside, worried the van might slide down into the ditch. Below him, he could see a small one-storey house, which he knew from Pete would be the landlords' place. They were an elderly couple, living on the same triangular piece of property as Pete and Cheryl, in a converted chicken coop. Connor's friends thought this was strange, but he didn't because he'd once rented a place that was a made-over dog kennel. It had been clear, even over the phone, that Pete didn't like the Greshners. "Fucking Chicken Man," he'd called the husband.

Connor's fingers were stiff from the cold and he was anxious to get into the house to thaw out, so he grabbed his suitcase from the back and started down the path. Immediately, a dog began barking. The yard light on the chicken coop came on and someone looked out the window of the door. Connor couldn't make out the face clearly, but the person seemed small, thin, and wore glasses with thick, dark frames. Connor waved a kind of hello, then heard Pete calling from the larger house, further down among the trees: "Hey, Connor. That you?"

Pete pulled him inside and slapped him on the shoulder. Connor took off the gloves to shake Pete's hand. "Jesus," Pete said. "You're cold as a bear turd in January."

The relief Connor felt at being in a warm place and finally at the end of his drive made him laugh. He thought he should make a joke about the broken heater, act like it hadn't really bothered him—maybe even say something about Frank. But all he could do was grin. "Well, I'm sure glad to be here," he said.

Though he hadn't seen Pete for two years, Connor noticed that his old pal didn't look much different. He'd cut his hair, but he still had the big moustache—the kind that looked like it would be always getting in your mouth. Connor had met Pete and his cousin, Glen, one summer when he was doing sheet-metal work, installing air ducts on a high-rise construction site. Pete and Glen were hired on as swampers, carrying stuff around for trades people and setting up sections of scaffolding. One afternoon Connor's boss, Murray, got the cousins to crawl inside several long sections of duct to seal the joints. The sealing compound smelled like airplane glue, and Connor was happy not to be cooped up inside the duct, breathing that crap, even with a mask. "Let those goofs do it,"

Murray told him. "I need you to have a clear head on this job." But they didn't seem to mind, even joked about how it was a cheap high. After work that night, Connor went with them to a bar, where Glen got into a fight with a couple of gay body-builders. Connor said Glen was lucky Pete hauled him out of that situation before he got his ass kicked. That's the way the cousins were: unpredictable, but full of energy.

Cheryl was in the living room on a couch facing a TV so small it looked like a toaster oven sitting on the coffee table. She held a large bag of pretzels in her lap and her eyes moved slowly from whatever program she'd been watching. "Hola, Connor," she said. "Good trip?" Cheryl had gained a bit of weight since he'd last seen her. She was wearing a kind of nylon sweatsuit, a style that was popular at the time with high-school kids, but she'd kept her long blonde hippie hair. Her eyes looked heavy, tired, and the air in the room was sharp with the tang of pot smoke. Connor leaned down to give her a kiss on the cheek—up close, she smelled a bit like old butter. On the TV, tiny people were arguing about something in some kind of an office, which caused Cheryl to laugh.

Pete motioned Connor to sit, and stood, rubbing his hands together. "Can I fix you a drink?" he asked. "Something hot?"

Connor realized he hadn't taken his coat off. "Sure. If it's no problem."

Pete laughed. "No such thing as a problem to us, hey Mama?" He looked at Cheryl who glanced over, nodded, then turned her attention back to the TV. "We are all about solutions, here, Connie." Connor hated to be called Connie—and Pete knew this about him—but he let it pass. As Pete went into the kitchen he shouted, "I saw the Chicken Man's light come on when you got here. Lucky he didn't set the German shepherd on you."

From the end table beside his chair, Connor picked up a framed photo of a newborn. "This your boy?"

Cheryl smiled. "That's the prince, all right. Down for the

count, thank God. I hope he doesn't wake you at night with his hollering; he's got Pete's vocal chords." For a moment, Connor had a funny picture in his mind of a child with a strangler's grip on Pete's throat, but he knew what she meant.

"Don't worry about me," he said. "I'll sleep like a baby."

After Connor had finished his hot rum, Pete looked at him and said, "You must be tired. I'll show you where you'll be bunking."

The truth was, Connor should have been exhausted but he felt more awake than when he'd got out of bed in the morning. Maybe it was the drink or being in a new place, or maybe something about the trip through the mountains and the snow. Whatever it was, he knew he wouldn't be able to sleep for a long while. They climbed up into an attic with a partition that made a small room at one end. "Well," Pete said, turning on the light, "here it is." Against one wall of the dark blue room stretched a narrow cot made up with clean sheets, wool blankets and a folded quilt. Opposite stood a dresser with a mirror and, under the single window, were two wooden chairs, one with no back.

Connor first thought it was a touch stark, but that it would do for the time being. From the broken chair he picked up an ashtray printed with a picture of a familiar, turquoise glacial lake and around its edge the words: Lake Louise, Alberta, Canada. "I won't be needing this; I quit last year," he said, and handed the ashtray to Pete.

"It's not ours," Pete said. "It was up here when we moved in. I found it in a box of stuff—some toys, kids' books, a tobacco tin full of crayons. Must have belonged to their daughter." Pete gestured with his chin toward the window, and Connor guessed that if he looked, he would be able to see the now-dark chicken coop through it. "Apparently she killed herself," Pete said. "They found her body floating up against the Brilliant dam."

Connor imagined the grieving Chicken Man and his wife hauling a soggy body from the debris floating at the edge of a cartoon dam. Then he realized Pete meant the more general "they"—those people, whoever they are, who accomplish such gruesome tasks regularly. Even though he didn't have children, Connor felt a sympathy for the old couple sleeping in the small house out there. "Suicide," he said. "Must be tough for the parents."

"From what I've been told, the Greshners don't accept that interpretation," Pete answered. "They insist it was an accident. But she probably couldn't stand being alive no more, having to deal with them every goddamn day of her life. They don't have any other kids." Pete looked at the ceramic souvenir in his hands. "I'll put it back in the box with the other things," he said. "And don't go saying anything to Chicken Man about living here, let me explain to him."

Connor wondered why Pete hadn't already told them he was coming, but he just nodded. On his way out, Pete stopped and turned around. "She was an adult," he said. "Not some little kid." As if that should have made it easier for the people she left behind.

Connor lay on his back in the dark for a long time that night, half wishing he hadn't quit smoking. He thought about the baby downstairs and the dead daughter of the people next door. He was glad he and Sandi hadn't had children. What had happened between them was complicated enough without kids thrown into the mix. Again, he went over the events of the evening she told him they were finished, and that he had become boring. "You don't want to do anything anymore," she said. They were sitting in the kitchen, the place they usually conducted serious conversations. He had made coffee for them, but Sandi wasn't drinking hers. Her slender fingers tapped the cup. She had had her hair streaked blonde and cut to fall into her face. Connor wondered how she could stand it.

"You sit around here listening to music, reading and complaining about the bullshit in the newspaper," she said. "Go to work and come home. That's it. Like you're broken but don't want to get fixed." She pushed the hair back and looked into his eyes. He couldn't return her gaze, turned his head. He wondered where she had got that notion, what it meant about him that he hadn't noticed himself. "It's not enough for me, Connor. I want to enjoy life."

"Movies," he said. "We go to movies." She just shook her head and looked at her untouched cup of coffee as if it, too, were a disappointment. But he couldn't deny her accusations. Over the past couple of years he'd grown less inclined to socialize. He'd said no to so many invitations that people had pretty well stopped asking. He was much happier in his own home, in the company of his wife. He told her that, and then she told him about Glen.

Connor was surprised to realize that more than anything he felt angry. At first he couldn't speak. He simply stared at Sandi—her turn to look away. His hands were shaking and he felt something physical—something angular and acidic—rise in him. He knew he had to get away from the house, from her. Without a word, he left the kitchen and grabbed his jacket. On the way out he slammed the door and heard one of the thin panes of glass break, but didn't stop. He walked for blocks and turned down the Drive, busy at this time of night on a Friday. Shoppers crowding the produce markets looking for the firmest tomatoes, the ripest avocadoes; people playing pool, drinking coffee. Life proceeding. Connor thought he should get a drink somewhere, like the aggrieved hero of some detective novel. But each time he came to a place that served alcohol, he kept walking. Outside a restaurant that also housed a small art gallery, a crowd of people who all seemed to know each other laughed and talked, maybe about the show inside. They had spilled out over the sidewalk and as he passed, he pushed his shoulder into the back of a shave-headed young guy dressed in black and entertaining two women with his wit. "Sorry," the young man said. Connor didn't even look at him—just kept moving. Then he thought he heard him say "asshole," though he couldn't be sure. Connor stopped and went back to him, stood as close as possible without actually touching him.

"What did you say?" Connor asked. Everything about the man facing him seemed like an act of affected aggression: the black string tie, silver collar tips on his shirt, and his spicy, too pungent cologne. Connor thought he smelled like a cinnamon stick. The people around them had grown silent and seemed to be watching in a haphazard way, as if this were some kind of arranged drama, intended to round off their evening. Connor was aware of what he must have looked like. Maybe the watchers thought he was drunk or one of those unpredictably bitter men who can be found on almost any city street but are normally easy to avoid. Connor ignored them and kept his focus on the guy in black.

"I said I was sorry," he answered. Connor watched as the man's eyes avoided his. He could see his adversary didn't have the look of commitment that would have made him dangerous. When Connor didn't respond, the guy added, "Isn't that good enough for you—since you bumped into me?"

It occurred to Connor it was his decision to make here, that however this situation would turn out was up to him. "Listen, cowboy," he said. "I'm going to give you a gift."

The man in black's brow contracted. "Cowboy?" he said.

"I'm going to accept your apology and continue on my way," Connor answered, and flicked the man's collar with his index finger. "Forget all about you." As Connor turned and moved down the block, the conversations began again, and though he imagined they were mostly about him, he didn't care.

Eventually, he walked long enough that his rage was taken over by a sadness of heart and the dread of impending loss. He realized that the outcome of the discussion with Sandi had already been clear in her mind. They hadn't sat down to come to a solution between the two of them; a third party was involved. She had handed Connor her resignation and there could be no real debate.

When he got home, he saw that she had cleaned up the broken glass and taped a plastic bread bag over the empty pane. She was still sitting at the kitchen table. She'd emptied and washed the coffee cups and set them side by side in the drying rack. To him, even the closeness of those empty cups suggested hypocrisy. Sandi had made herself a mug of herbal tea, possibly to calm herself. And maybe it had worked because she appeared almost tranquil, as if this were simply a problem to solve. She held her cup in both hands. "Are you okay?" she asked.

"Don't think it's going to be so easy."

Her expression changed slightly, her mouth tightened. "What does that mean?"

"I won't stand in your way," he said, and sat across from her. Back where they'd started the evening. "But it isn't going to be easy. You can't take a marriage apart like an old sweater."

They talked then as if they were negotiating a business deal, which he realized they were, in a sense. She said she didn't want any of the furniture, that it suited him more, as if the chairs, tables, their bed, everything they'd chosen together, had become some kind of symbol of their shared life—grown unbearable to her.

Connor woke to the unmistakable smell of burnt toast and the sound of a baby crying. Through the window, which had no curtain, he could see a snarled network of branches and behind them, an overcast sky. Then, a wave of sunlight moved across the branches, illuminating them against the grey, and he suddenly felt happy, as if the first day in this new life were sending him a sign. But just as quickly as the light had appeared, it shadowed over again, and the world outside the window seemed more gloomy than it had before. He felt disappointed but not dispirited. He decided that he could hold onto that brilliant moment if he chose.

When he came into the kitchen, Cheryl was holding the baby and looking out the window into the yard at the back of the house. Her blouse was unbuttoned, but not open, and he figured she'd been feeding the baby, who had the stunned appearance of someone who'd drunk himself full. Cheryl turned and smiled at him.

"Morning, Connor. Or is it closer to afternoon?" She made a point of looking at the clock on the stove. "I guess there's no need to ask if you slept all right," she said. "Help yourself to coffee. There's porridge in that pot and bread if you want toast."

"Toast and coffee will be great, thanks," he said, and took a mug from among several hanging on hooks under the cupboard. "Where's Pete?"

"Outside somewhere," she answered. She did up her buttons, unself-consciously. "I heard him talking to Greshner, earlier. At least they weren't shouting."

Connor liked Cheryl. She seemed like a person whose wants and the means to achieve them were all easily managed. She came from a small town in Saskatchewan and had a kind of open, prairie-flower face he liked to think was common among people from that part of the world. He guessed that having the baby had taken something out of her because she looked a touch tired and worn out. Even so, from where he stood she appeared to be happy with what she had.

"Here," she said, standing and raising her son toward him. "Do you mind holding Jesse for a moment?"

So that was his name, Connor thought. He took the child carefully in his hands. He didn't have much experience with babies, but knew he was supposed to support the head.

"I'll be right back," she said, then left him in the kitchen with her little wispy-haired child. The two of them stared at each other—Connor imagining the baby was certain this new adult represented some form of bad luck. Connor had a strange feeling that he didn't like Jesse, though he wasn't sure at first why, and this emotion surprised him. He thought the child had a sour little face, and the crescent-shaped rash above his upper lip made him appear mildly unhealthy. But when he looked closer at the mouth, the bow-like shape of it and the round chin underneath, he understood what he was responding to. This small baby, who'd done him no harm, bore enough of a resemblance to Glen that Connor had unconsciously become predisposed against him. At the same moment, Jesse screwed up his face and began to howl. Unsure of what to do next, Connor wondered if the child had read his mind.

"Ssh, hey, hey," Connor said, which if anything only turned up the volume a notch. Fortunately, Cheryl came back and quickly took the baby. "Don't worry," she said, possibly interpreting the look on Connor's face as one of apology. "He doesn't seem to like strangers much. I'm surprised he lasted as long as he did." She made the comforting sounds of a mother and stuck the tip of her little finger between Jesse's lips, which soon reversed the effect Connor had had on him.

When Pete came in a few minutes later, the boy was asleep and Connor was drinking his coffee. Pete wore a quilted, red plaid shirt and flared corduroy pants. Connor thought he looked as if he'd just arrived from another era, and considered making a joke about Pete's sartorial choices, but decided he might not find the comments funny. He didn't want to establish a wrong-foot atmosphere in his new home. Pete sat next to Cheryl with his own mug of coffee and poured a handful of sugar into it before taking a drink. "I had a pleasant conversation with Chicken Man this morning," he said, looking first at his wife, then at Connor. Pete licked a few drops of coffee from his moustache, then laughed, as if he'd said something humorous. "He was pretty curious about your van up there on the road, but I didn't tell him much. Let the nosy bastard wonder—none of his business anyway, right?" He glanced at Cheryl, who nodded without taking her attention from the baby asleep in her lap.

"Now, Connor," he hollered, and the baby jerked at the sound of his roaring voice. "I figure we'll drive into town today, and I'll show you around."

On the way in, Pete had Connor swing past the Church of Christ the Evangelist, where Pete kept up the grounds and did general maintenance. The church was a dour barn-shaped structure that had been painted dark brown with white trim and featured a stark, white cross at its peak. It cast its shade over a smaller, flat-roofed building with a chain-link fence around it. On this one, the colour scheme had been reversed. Silhouettes of lambs frolicking, apparently cut from plywood and painted the same brown as the church, had been fastened along one wall. "I didn't know you were religious," Connor said.

"I was damn lucky to get this job," Pete answered, pointing toward the plain wooden doors at the entryway, as if they offered some elucidation on what he'd said. "Actually, no one around here would touch it. Seems there's been some controversy about behaviour in the daycare."

"Hard to find work here?" Connor asked, ignoring the issue Pete had raised. Connor hadn't considered the possibility of unemployment. His plan was to settle in for a few weeks, then once he had a good sense of the town, to get some kind of job and let his new life unfold from there. He'd imagined himself framing houses or doing some other kind of construction work against the backdrop of the Interior mountains.

"Christ, yeah," Pete said. "I hope you've got some savings to fall back on." Then he grinned and punched Connor on the shoulder. "But, you know, I found this gig, so it ain't impossible." Pete waved at nothing and pointed away from the church. "Let's get the hell out of here," he said. As far as Connor could tell, he intended no irony.

Over the next few weeks, Connor devoted himself to learning Nelson as if it were a college course he'd enrolled in. He borrowed a history of the area from the library. He took the Chamber of Commerce walking tour, and at Lakeside Park, talked to an old-timer scanning the beach with a metal detector, who told him of secret tunnels beneath Nelson's sidewalks. All these things he could do, but he couldn't find a job.

One afternoon, on his way home from a drive along the north shore, he stopped at the Heritage Inn for a beer. He bought a pint at the bar and headed up to the pub's top level where it was usually quiet during the day. And there, in a corner by a window, reading the local newspaper, sat the hitchhiker he'd picked up on his trip from the coast.

"Hey, Frank," Connor said. "How'd you end up here?"

Frank folded the paper and smiled. "Thumb power," he said. "And good-natured motorists. How's the big change going?"

Connor blushed, remembering all the talking he'd done along that stretch of highway. "Well, no significant achievements as yet, but I like being in this new place."

"You still with those friends?" Frank asked. He fished a cigarette from the pack of Black Cats on the table, and shoved the pack toward Connor.

"No thanks," Connor said. "Yeah. I might be there a while; it seems the job situation around here is pretty bad."

Frank nodded. "Know how to use a hammer?"

"I'm no carpenter, but I've spent enough time on construction sites that I figure I can handle most things."

"My brother-in-law's building an addition on his house. In Ymir. It's only about a week's work, and he can't pay much, but we could use an extra pair of hands," Frank said.

Connor raised his arms above his head and shook them like a believer in a revival tent. "I'm your loyal servant," he said.

They talked for a good part of the afternoon, although Connor realized again that he contributed most of the conversation. But he felt comfortable with Frank and didn't notice anything in Frank's responses that suggested he ought to shut up.

Eventually, he told the whole story of the split with Sandi, how Glen and Pete fit into the picture, and how, more than anything, he felt betrayed. He explained how whenever he had this kind of feeling, his anger took on a black-and-white nature. "I felt ransacked," Connor said. "And I just decided to close a door between us."

Frank looked curious but not judgemental. He set his beer on the table, then spoke. "My grandfather used to say: 'If you always react the same way to life's situations, you'll never get ahead.' He was a smart old bugger."

On his drive home, Connor considered the notion that bumping into Frank again was a portent of good luck. The money didn't matter so much as the feeling he suddenly had of possibility. The rich bright blue of the sky reflected his emotions. As he parked along the road, he noticed the open doors on the garage at the top of the drive. On his way down to the house he peered into the dark of the garage. The light inside was dim, but he could make out a workbench along the back wall, and rows of tools hung carefully along the side walls.

"Can I help you?" The voice came from behind Connor,

and made him jump. He turned to face a short man with dark lips, wispy grey hair and a pair of glasses that made his eyes appear unnaturally large. Chicken Man, he thought. He realized that in the three weeks he'd been living on this property, he'd never come face to face with his landlords.

"Actually, I'm staying with Pete and Cheryl, in the house." Connor motioned down the path.

"Yes, I know who you are and where you are living," said the older man. "I've seen you. But you haven't come even to say hello, have you? And now, perhaps you're looking for something in my garage."

"Listen," said Connor. "You're right. I've been rude. I apologize." Then he introduced himself, and the old man told him his name was Hans Greshner. Greshner held a digging fork and had obviously been working in the vegetable garden near the smaller house.

"How's the gardening around here?" Connor asked, though he'd never had any interest in growing plants, indoors or out.

Greshner pulled a handkerchief from his back pocket and blew his nose with one hand, then tucked the handkerchief away again. "Are you a gardener, Mr. Connor, or are you simply making meaningless conversation?"

"All I know about gardening is that it involves plants and dirt, but I am curious." Connor grinned. "Never too old to learn, eh?"

Greshner shook his head, then turned back to the garden, motioning Connor to follow him. The old man walked with quick steps, his shoulders hunched as if he might dive forward at any moment. He bent stiffly to grab a handful of soil and held it toward Connor. "It has taken me a long time to get this earth so dark and rich. This is the key: a good base to build your garden on."

Building a garden—an interesting concept, Connor thought. Greshner held forth on the topic of gardening while Connor listened. He could understand how someone—Pete, for example—might take a disliking to the old man. He gave the impression of being impatient, maybe slightly angry or arrogant, but if you gave him the benefit of the doubt, you could just as easily accept these things as his style. Overlook his presentation and hear what he was saying.

Eventually, Greshner looked at his watch, then up at the darkening sky. "Well," he said, "now I've done so much talking, there's no time left for working." He knocked the dirt from the digging fork with the side of his shoe. "Would you like to come in for a cup of tea?"

"Sure," Connor said. "Too dark to plant corn."

"Ha," Greshner said, and led the way. "Aren't you the comic one? By the way, don't worry about the dog. She's in her kennel, around back." He opened the door and shouted into the house, "Octavia, we have a guest—Mr. Connor, the fellow staying in the old house with Peter and Cheryl."

Inside, Connor saw there was no need to shout; the house was tiny. Apparently, Pete's claim that it was made-over chicken coops was right. The entrance was in a small sitting area, with two stuffed chairs and reading lamps. Beyond was a narrow kitchen, and on the other side of that a door leading, he imagined, to the bedroom. Mrs. Greshner, Octavia, sat at the kitchen table, sewing a button on a faded work shirt. She finished her stitch, snipped the thread, and smiled. "Hello, Mr. Connor. So nice to meet you." She stood to shake his hand. Connor was surprised at how diminutive she was. Even shorter than Hans, and fine-boned. Her hand in his felt like a child's.

Hans washed up at the sink as Octavia plugged in the kettle and set out a plate of homemade cookies. Even the cookies were small, Connor thought—not much bigger around than his watch face—and suddenly he felt oversized and oafish.

Some time later, Octavia brought out a large photo album to show Connor what the place looked like when she and Hans had lived in the larger house. There were photos of the coops when they had housed chickens, shots of the garden, and one of a dark-haired Hans holding a saw beside a pile of lumber, taken, as far as Connor could tell, where the garage now stood. And then in one picture, Octavia stood in front of the house with a small girl at her side, the girl's hands buried deep in the pockets of her coat. The girl had the same fine features as the woman, but wore glasses, and Connor realized this must be their daughter. Before Connor could comment, Hans pointed to the photo and said, "That is our daughter, Liesl. Only six years old, then."

Connor cleared his throat. Normally, he would have asked about her, but after what Pete had told him, he wasn't sure what to say. "Cute kid," he said, finally, hoping that would be neutral enough.

"We haven't seen her for a long time," Hans said, sitting straight and stiff in his chair. "We aren't sure exactly what happened to her."

Octavia closed the album gently and glanced at her husband. "Maybe we will look at this again another time," she said.

The kitchen was quiet then as they finished their tea, and Connor could hear cars travelling past on the road above. He set his empty cup on the table. "I should get going," he said, and stood. "You folks would probably like to get to your dinner."

Pete was sitting in the living room reading a *National Geographic* when Connor came in. Pete held out the magazine towards Connor. "It says here the Great Barrier Reef is disappearing. Too much shit in the ocean." He tossed the magazine on the coffee table and leaned forward. "So, Chicken Man finally cornered you?" Pete asked.

Connor wondered how long Pete had been sitting here, waiting to interrogate him. The thought made him angry, but he spoke carefully. "They're not so bad, Pete. The old man has a peculiar style, but if you let that go, you can talk to him."

"You were in their house a long time," Pete said. He picked up the magazine again and began flipping through it. "What did you talk about?"

"We had tea," Connor said, "and yapped about nothing. But I did have some good luck today." Pete looked up at him. "I bumped into a guy in the Heritage—the hitchhiker I picked up on the way here."

"The Indian guy?"

"Yeah. He offered me some work, rough carpentry. With him and his brother-in-law."

Pete snorted. "Quite a day for you, huh? Get set up with a bunch of Indians and spend the afternoon in the coop shooting the shit with Chicken Man and his old lady." Pete shook his head with the look of someone who has lost faith in another. "We better go see what's for supper," he said. "Before you have any more good luck."

The following Friday, Connor came home from working with Frank. They'd spent three days so far on the extension, and had finished putting the roof up, so they quit early. His arms were sore from all the lifting and hammering, but Connor felt happy. Frank was a pleasure to work with: methodical and careful, but he had a subtle sense of humour Connor appreciated. The brother-in-law had given Connor five $20 bills, saying he might need something for the weekend, and Connor thought he would take Pete and Cheryl out for supper.

As he walked from the road, he could hear shouting and the dog barking. He ran down the path to the yard of the old house, where he saw Octavia holding back the German shepherd. The dog snarled and lunged toward Pete and Hans, facing each other. Cheryl stood behind Pete, holding the baby in one arm and pulling on the tail of Pete's shirt with the other. Everyone was hollering. The afternoon sun shone down, illuminating the scene like a weird dramatic tableau. The fresh green of new leaves on the aspens and poplars around the yard created a vivid and fragrant backdrop, out of sync with the variety of emotion unfolding there.

"You fucking Nazi," Pete shouted. "Who let you into this country in the first place?" He had his hand around the wrist of the old man, who spluttered and yelled, "God damn you," as he struggled to keep his footing.

Connor tried to get between the two men. "Pete," he said. "Stop this. Calm down." He felt a punch intended for Pete hit him on the back of his neck, and he turned. "Jesus, Hans, settle down." He looked at Cheryl. "What's going on here?"

But before she could answer, the old man yelped—a sound that reminded Connor of wood splitting—and fell onto his side. Connor grabbed Pete and shoved him back toward the door of the house. All he could think of to say was "stop it, stop it," and he held Pete until he could feel the anger in the man ease up. He watched the dark rage that contorted Pete's face dissolve slowly, and saw that they both knew something irreversible had taken place.

When things quieted down, Connor helped Hans back home and made certain the old man was physically okay, no bones broken, before leaving him. Connor couldn't get a straight response from Hans about what had taken place, and Octavia was clearly upset and concerned for her husband, so he didn't ask her about the incident. "I'll come back later, to check on Hans," he said.

Pete had taken his truck and roared away while Connor was with the Greshners, but he found Cheryl sitting in the kitchen, rocking Jesse. He got himself a glass of water and realized his hands were shaking. He could see Cheryl had been crying, so he sat across from her and waited for her to speak.

"He got laid off today," she said, eventually. "The old man'd been bugging him about the rent. So what—we were a little behind. Pete told him he'd get everything owed to him. But the old man just wouldn't leave him alone. That, and those self-righteous so-called Christians at that church. It wasn't his fault."

Connor wasn't sure if she were referring to the fight with Greshner or whatever it was that had got Pete fired. "I can understand that Pete had a good reason to be pissed," he said. He wanted to tell her that it hadn't been a smart thing to go after the old man, but he kept the thought to himself.

Cheryl finally looked at him; she wasn't smiling. "You're very understanding, aren't you?" she said. "I mean, you certainly seem to understand the Greshners real well."

"Cheryl, I'm not taking sides in this, I just ..." He let the sentence hang there, unfinished.

"Maybe you better not say anything else," she said, and turned back to her baby. "I think I'd like to be alone a while."

Connor wasn't sure what to do next; all the certainty he'd felt earlier was suddenly gone. He nodded, went up to his room and sat on the cot. He knew that even if he wanted to, he wouldn't be welcome to stay there any longer, and so began packing. When he was done he put the five twenties in an envelope and left it on the bed, though he'd already given Pete and Cheryl a cheque for the month's room and board. On his way out, he looked for her in the kitchen, but saw that she was lying on the living-room couch, tucked in, asleep, under a blanket with the baby.

Connor's intention was to get away from that place, but he saw lights on in the Greshners' house, and remembered his promise to check on them. He knocked lightly on the front door. After a moment, Octavia looked out through the curtain, her face tense and sharp, then unlocked and let him in. "Is Hans okay?" he asked.

The old man came out from the bedroom. "Of course I'm

okay," he said. "It's going to take a lot more than that punk to put me out of commission." But Connor could see a shade of fear in his eyes. Hans wore his housecoat, and Connor noticed a dark bruise on his arm above his wrist.

"I don't think you need to worry about Pete tonight," Connor said. He explained that he wouldn't be staying in the other house, but offered to sleep in the van up on the roadway, if it would make them feel safer.

"It's not necessary," Octavia said. "But thank you."

"Do you have somewhere else you can go?" Hans asked.

"Yeah, I've got some friends in town," Connor answered. Before he left, he told the Greshners he'd call them the next morning, first thing. On the way to his van, Connor figured he'd ask if he could stay with Frank and his brother-in-law for a day or two, and if that didn't work out, he'd get a motel room. Up on the road, he smelled woodsmoke from the chimney of the small house below him. He pictured the old couple there, curled together on their bed, keeping each other warm. Safe. Trying not to think about Pete. Trying not to think about their daughter.

He laughed at how things had gone, how his fantasy of inventing a great new life had so far turned out to be not much more than that—fantasy. It was a strange thing that the most solid people in all this drama—the Greshners—were the ones who'd lost the most. And somehow they managed to find a way through their lives, day after day.

Even stranger that he suddenly felt happy, full of hope, as if some cloudiness had lifted from his thoughts. And this realization increased his joy. Nothing was certain, but that wasn't important. A dog barked somewhere and he smiled down into the trees and climbed into his van for the trip to town.

A Thing of Beauty

Marek was well into a rant on the nature of significance—one he'd delivered variations of countless times—when his attention snagged on the grain of the plywood behind Tomas's head. "Take that sheet of good-one-side on the wall," he said. "If you squint a bit and lean to the right, you can almost see the image of a Madonna. Now, that's what I'm talking about."

Jacinthe reached for Marek's pint of beer. The house draught—no designer brew for him. "You're finished with this, my good man," she said. "As soon as you see the Virgin Mary in the wallpaper, you're cut off. Good thing we took a cab." Tomas and Elaine laughed along with her.

This bothered Marek. He liked to be the joker, but didn't

much care for the role of jok-ee. He'd insisted they ride out to this pub in Surrey, half under construction and, as far as the others were concerned, gloomy as a burned-out bus station on a winter night. "This is real," he proclaimed. "Salt of the earth." He swung his long arms out toward the bleak cavern of the hotel drinking room. "These people are genuine. No yuppie posturing in a made-over warehouse; no twelve-year-old single malt with water imported from some Norwegian glacier."

"Oh yeah, they're real all right," Jacinthe said. Marek saw her glance toward the pool tables where a half dozen large-bellied men, a slurry of beards, denim and creased leather, hollered and swaggered over pitchers of beer in an endless game of eight ball, their Harleys parked in a row just outside the bar entrance. "Real dangerous." The birthmark that stained her cheek had darkened slightly through the make-up she'd put on it. He loved the mark, the way it contrasted with her pale complexion, her cornflower blue eyes. Whenever he thought about the effort she made to lighten the blemish with powders or creams, all the while affecting an attitude of not caring, he suddenly felt the fins of a deep tenderness swim through him.

"It's funny in a way," Elaine said. "Here we are in Vancouver for a hit of *city*, and we end up in a pub that's not even as nice as the sleaziest bar back home."

Marek ignored her; if it weren't for Tomas, he wouldn't have kept up his friendship with this couple. And he'd almost written off Tomas, despite their years as friends and co-workers, when he had moved in with Elaine. Later, Marek had felt abandoned after Tomas quit his job at the sawmill to sign on with Elaine's dream of small-town domesticity. Marek saw their leaving Vancouver as evidence of a fundamental deficiency. "At least you know where you stand with those guys," he said, pointing in the direction of the pool players. "You don't fuck with them, they leave you alone. Notice that they're not trying to sell us anything, or asking us to vote for them."

Tomas, ever the conciliator, seemed to recognize Marek's seriousness. "I guess it's a side of the city we don't usually acknowledge. Hey, Elaine and I are tourists this week, so let's tour. Indeed, here's to touring," he said, and raised his glass.

"But Jacinthe is right," Elaine said. Marek could see she wasn't going to let this one rest—knew it by the way she narrowed her deep-set eyes and tucked in her pudgy chin as she spoke. "Excuse me for saying this, but it's precisely things like biker gangs and drug crimes that we wanted to get away from when we moved to the Okanagan." She turned to Marek. "What if, God forbid, one of these so-called real men were to grab Caitlyn on her way to kindergarten one morning? Do you think you'd be so accepting then?"

"In the first place," Marek said, "it won't happen. We always take her to school ourselves." He raised his hand against her intended response. "You simply have to understand the risks and eliminate them. Same thing anywhere you go. I've been around long enough not to do anything stupid. And if some half-witted bastard does mess with me or my family, it's their ass that's in serious trouble."

Tomas spoke in a mock German accent: "Marek knows vere ze bodies can be buried, ja?"

Marek finished his beer and stood. "All I'm saying is I think I know how to handle myself." He turned to Elaine and bowed slightly. "Now, if you'll excuse me, I'm off to the can to do just that."

As Marek unzipped at the urinal, two of the men from the pool tables came into the washroom. The taller one was speaking, "… just about crapped my drawers," and his partner roared. They stepped up to the porcelain.

"A waste of good beer," Marek said.

The two turned their heads toward him. "What's that?"

asked the shorter one. His gut hung over his belt as if it were trying to escape.

"You know, drink it down out there, then come in here and piss it out," Marek said.

"That's the fucking point."

"Yeah, I guess you're right," said Marek. His laughter felt a touch too loud.

The short one said to his pal, "What I tell ya, Kenny? Ain't I always right?"

"You look like a man whose word is pretty much gospel," Marek said, and this time they all laughed.

"I see what you mean," answered Kenny, his tarnished teeth grinning through a tangle of wiry black facial hair. "Even this civilian recognizes your brilliance."

Maybe it was the way the word *civilian* bit into him, or maybe it was the beer and the conversation Marek had just come from, but his next sentence leapt from his mouth before he had a chance to consider it. He asked, "You fellas wouldn't know where I could get a handgun?"

Kenny and the shorter man looked at each other. "Why would you be asking us a question like that?" Kenny said. "Go to a gun store."

"What the fuck do you want with a *handgun*?" the shorter one asked, pronouncing the word as if it were from a foreign language.

"I know how to use one," Marek said. "I've taken a target pistol course."

"Kenny," the short one said. "Man says he's taken a course. Should have recognized that right up front, way he managed his dick."

Kenny laughed, which cinched Marek's resolve. "Okay, maybe I made a mistake; maybe you aren't the right guys to ask." Marek backed away. "I guess I misjudged you—my apologies." He started for the door.

"Hold on a sec, partner," said the short one. "If we were the right guys, how much would you be thinking to pay for this merchandise?"

"I've got a hundred bills, cash, in my pocket."

"Sandwich money, my man."

"Like I said, maybe I made a poor assessment of the situation." Marek waited this time, smiling, friendly as if he'd just asked them for the time.

The short one thought it over for a moment, while Kenny watched Marek. Then Short Man looked up. "You gonna be around a while?"

"How long?" Marek asked. He was enjoying this moment.

"Give us half an hour and we'll see if we can't fix you up."

It was over an hour later and Marek's companions were long past wanting to leave, wondering why he insisted on staying, when he noticed Short Man and Kenny come back into the bar through the lobby door. They looked toward Marek and nodded in the direction of the men's room. He'd been waiting for them so long, he almost kicked the table over getting to his feet. "All right," he said to Jacinthe, "I'll be right back and then we can go. I'll call for a taxi on my way."

"No," she said. "You hurry up and I'll get the cab."

In the washroom, Short Man asked for the money, which Marek carefully counted out from his wallet. Then Kenny reached inside his jacket and handed Marek the pistol. The chrome plating along its barrel was scratched and worn off in places, the hand grip wrapped with black hockey tape. The gun was smaller than Marek had imagined it would be, but it felt heavy in his hand. "Does it work?"

"You're going to have to trust us on that," said Short Man. "For a measly hundred, it don't come with bullets."

"What make is it?" Marek asked.

Short Man laughed. "Fucking no-name brand," he said, folding Marek's bills into his jeans pocket. "Wal-mart brand."

All the way back in the cab, Marek felt the heft of his new acquisition until he could barely keep shut about it. He sat up front with the driver and the two of them talked non-stop about taxes, road rage and the state of the country. The evening was warm for November, and Jacinthe suggested walking the last five blocks to the house. As they got out of the car, Marek had to ask her for money to pay the fare.

"I thought you went to the bank machine this afternoon," she said. Marek shrugged.

They walked along the sidewalk in pairs, the men ahead of the women. Tomas asked, "So, have they bumped you up to foreman yet?"

Marek glanced at Tomas, then away. "The place is still a hotbed of ass-kissing. I'll be driving that forklift till I drop. Or, till Barkley falls into a chipper," he said. With each step, the gun in his jacket pocket bumped lightly against his leg. "You were only the first of the good people to leave."

Tomas cleared his throat, then said, "You and Jacinthe ever think about moving out of this place? Maybe try the Okanagan?"

Marek didn't bother to answer.

On the next block, they passed a house with a blue plastic tarp covering half the roof, which reminded Tomas of the final stage of renovations they'd had done on their place in Vernon. "At one point, I thought we'd be living with a tarp over our heads for the next twenty years," he said.

"But you know," Elaine spoke, and Marek thought her voice had grown even whinier on the ride home, "we never worried about leaving tools or building supplies out in the yard overnight."

Jacinthe said, "It sounds like paradise."

"You should come visit," Elaine said. "You can see for yourself how beautiful it is."

Then, under a streetlight, Marek finally drew the gun from his pocket and stopped them all. "This, too, proves my point," he said, thrusting the weapon into the air between them.

"Jesus Christ." Elaine almost swallowed her tongue.

"Marek, where did you get that?" Jacinthe asked.

"Do you understand that this sad machine, with its no doubt equally miserable history, also has an exquisiteness?" Marek said.

"Sometimes you go too far," Jacinthe said. He could imagine the blood rushing to her cheeks, the birthmark shining darkly in the even darker night. She brushed past him, turned and began to walk quickly toward their home, then called back, "I don't want that thing in my house. And don't you dare let Caitlyn see it."

Elaine was with her almost immediately, shaking her head as if her suspicions had been confirmed. Even Tomas, smiling weakly, appeared upset. "Not one of your best ideas," he said.

Marek woke with a squirrel in his chest. Morning light pounded his eyes; his tongue was a sea urchin trapped in a tidal pool. Jacinthe was already up; he could hear her laughing with Caitlyn downstairs. He guessed they were playing Snakes and Ladders, Caitlyn's latest passion. She loved to scrutinize the tiny morality scenes pictured around the board. Her favourite pair began at the tail end of a snake, and showed a freckle-faced girl pulling a cat's tail; the snake's head, to which the unlucky player descended, had the child on the ground, crying and holding up a severely scratched arm. This was something she knew about. "Not supposed to hurt kitties, right, Daddy?" she'd asked. He'd nodded solemnly and thought how much her eyes looked like Jacinthe's.

Marek got up and took the gun from the back of his sock drawer. He lay in bed with it under his pillow, trying to find the certainty he'd felt when buying the gun and, at the same time, half dreaming of its beauty. Tomas's voice, and Elaine's, rose from the kitchen, then they were gone.

He eventually succumbed to the pistol's attraction and was aiming it around the room, sighting down the barrel like a boy, when Jacinthe came in. "I don't want to know how much you spent on that thing and I absolutely will not listen to any speeches about its dignity or whatever," she said. She stood in the doorway with her arms crossed. Marek patted the bed beside him, but she wouldn't budge. "I'm serious," she said.

Before he could answer, Caitlyn came running into the room. She grabbed her mother's leg, swung toward the bed and suddenly stopped. "What's that, Daddy?"

And Marek admitted that Jacinthe was right.

When he came home that evening, he entered through the garage, and quietly locked the heavily weighted paper bag in the bottom of his tool box. They'd agreed that he couldn't just throw the gun into a dumpster. Some bottle scrounger—or worse, a couple of kids—might find it and get into trouble. "What about a bridge?" Jacinthe had asked. "You walk out to the middle of the Lions Gate Bridge and drop it into the inlet."

Marek had parked and carried his small bundle halfway across to the North Shore. But as he stood against the wind funnelling up through the narrows, the rough iron-coloured water below him, he realized he couldn't so simply destroy this thing. It felt too selfish, too wasteful. He drove around for hours with the package tucked under his spare tire in the trunk, trying to conjure up a suitable end for the handgun. Finally, he went home without a plan, only a notion that a solution would surely come to him if he gave it enough time.

Jacinthe was in the kitchen, elegant in her preparation of a Mediterranean feast he knew she intended to heal any wounds left from his waving of the gun in their guests' faces. "Well?" she said, poised over garlic and black olives.

He took several pieces of red pepper from a plate near her elbow. "Done," he said. "Tomas and Elaine back yet?"

"They took Caitlyn to the playground. They used our card and rented a video for tonight. From a Henry James novel—no violence." She laughed and waited for his response. When he didn't answer, she set her hands on the counter. "Marek …"

"I'm just not feeling great," he said. He offered her a slice of pepper. She shook her head, so he bit into it. "I'll go wash up and then help you in here."

Later, they ate pasta and drank large glasses of bright Chianti; Marek joked and lectured as usual. Nobody mentioned the night before or the gun, but he knew they were all thinking about it. He knew that Tomas and Elaine would go home and eventually the whole incident would become an anecdote for them, a testimonial to verify that this trip to the city had been fruitful. Jacinthe wouldn't question him about it again. It would be as if forgotten. Only he would be left with the weight of the package locked away in the garage. Only he would feel the burden of its beauty.

The End of Water

I was hanging around the snack bar, learning to blow smoke rings, when Mike Davis walked in wearing a uniform. Nash, squinting through black horn-rims, spotted him first and said to me, "Hey Wheeler, isn't that your bodyguard?" which threw Scottie off the tabletop drum riff he had going. He'd played the Ventures' "Wipe Out" on the jukebox for about the hundredth time that morning and was using his fingers as drumsticks on the edge of the table. I set my cigarette in the ashtray, and turned around to look.

I was surprised to see Mike in a uniform; he was the last guy I would have expected to join the air force. Two years had passed since the end of Grade 9 when we'd gone on to different high schools, and though I occasionally thought of him, I hadn't bothered to look him up. We'd been close friends at one time but over the years had simply drifted apart.

Scottie asked, "What do you mean, bodyguard?" I knew what Nash meant, but Scottie and Gwyn, who was sitting beside me, didn't have a clue. They hadn't been on this base long enough.

"A few years ago anyone who bothered Wheeler had to deal with Mousie Davis," Nash said.

"Mousie? Wow, he sounds like trouble," Scottie said, half-assed keeping up his finger-drumming. I could see he was watching and evaluating, trying to fit this new character into his spectrum of toughness.

Mike Davis didn't look like much of a hardrock. Certainly not to Scottie, who was already over six feet and spent a lot of time in the weight room at the back of the rec centre. Mike was only average height and slim. But he was like one of those scrub maples that grew out along the sand dunes—hard as iron—and afraid of nothing. He'd got the nickname when he first came to our school, a farmer's kid among the military brats. He wasn't big then, either, and a brylcreemed troll named Eddy Knight took an instant dislike to him. For some reason he gave him the name Mousie, and by the end of the week, only the teachers were calling him Mike. On Friday morning, Eddy started in on him, asking if his dad was a cheese farmer. Mousie got up from his desk, walked over to the smirking bully, and without any hesitation punched him in the head half a dozen times, then went back to his seat.

They had to take Eddy to the base hospital, there was so much blood. Mike was suspended for a week, and from then on, people only used the name Mousie behind his back. That wasn't the end of his troubles. But I never saw him back down from a fight, and as far as I knew, he never lost one that was fair.

"Hey, Air Force," I shouted, and Mike turned around. He didn't seem to recognize me at first, but then his face shifted into that familiar half smile. He paid for his coffee and came over to our table. He looked a bit uncomfortable in his khaki uniform—summer colours—with the wedge cap tucked under an epaulette.

"Hi, Wheeler," he said. "Long time, eh? Mind if I sit with you guys?"

"Join us, man," I said, and moved over to let him pull up a chair. I gestured toward the others. "Mike," I said, "you remember Nash; this is Scottie and Gwyn." Gwyn and I had been going steady since Christmas. I could see the string around her neck that I knew held my signet ring—a silver W set into a rectangle of black diamond. The ring hung down between her breasts, which so far she'd only let me touch on the outside of her bra. I often imagined what pleasures might be under the lace, and dreamed of the day I'd find out.

I'd known Gwyn since elementary school in Saskatoon, when she was just the skinny red-haired girl at the end of the block. Eventually, her dad had been transferred to Germany and my family went to Prince Edward Island. We moved back to the prairies a few years later and had been here since. When Gwyn showed up at school in September, I was stunned by the changes in her. She was pretty, smart and more sophisticated than anyone I'd ever met.

She also had no difficulty expressing whatever was on her mind. "So, Mike," she said, "what's this about you being Wheeler's bodyguard?"

Mike shrugged and looked down at his hands.

"When did you join the military?" I asked. His shoulder patch said Air Craftsman 1, the rank of the most lowly recruit, so I knew it couldn't have been long before.

"I quit school in December," he said, staring directly at Gwyn, as if he were challenging her to comment on dropouts. "I had to get my dad's permission to sign up." He looked at her until she turned away.

She reached over and began to play with the hairs on my

forearm. "Your dad let you quit school?" she asked. Her father was always on her case about going to university and making something of herself. Which suited her; she had dreams of being the first person in her family with a degree and often talked about the interesting life she imagined would follow this accomplishment. My own parents would have offered me as a human sacrifice before they'd give me permission to drop out.

"He wanted me to work on the farm with him, but we don't get along all that well," Mike said.

We talked a while until Scottie reminded Nash they had baseball practice, and Mike said he should probably get back to the barracks.

About a week later, Mike showed up at my house in a black Mercury Meteor I recognized as his dad's old car, and asked if I wanted to go for a ride. My old lady was pretty charmed by the new Mike. She'd never been too happy with the idea of me spending time with a farmer, but now that he'd joined the forces she seemed to think he'd been transformed. Maybe she hoped he would set me on the right path—the one that led to officer training. But as soon as we were out of sight of the house, he told me to reach under the seat and fix us each a barley sandwich. Same old Mike.

He turned onto the road that led away from the base and into town, and I knew we were going to the bridge that crosses the Assiniboine River. I handed him a beer, then opened one for myself, took a long, gulping drink and set the bottle between my legs. I asked, "What's it like being in the air force?"

"Well, it's not as bad as you might think. I guess the worst part is being on the bottom of the shit heap," he answered. "I can drink legally in the Airmen's club and they even give us free safes: 'Prophylactics are a man's second-best friend,' according to the med corporal." This sounded weird coming from Mike; as long as I'd known him, he'd never had a girlfriend. He'd always seemed socially clumsy, especially around the opposite sex.

"I may need to get some of those from you one of these days," I said.

"Yeah?" He looked at me, and I tried to look casual.

"Things are getting pretty heavy with Gwyn and me," I said. "She's all over me—hot for my bod." I don't know why I said this. The lie seemed to come from a part of me I couldn't control, but once the words were in the air there was no reclaiming them, even though I felt I had somehow hurt Gwyn.

Mike parked in the gravel on the south side of the crossing—where only a few years earlier we would have left our bicycles—and we walked out to the middle of the bridge deck. Just like in the old days, we climbed over the rail and underneath to sit on the concrete support. We opened two more beers and tossed the caps down into the moving water.

He pointed to where a back eddy had eaten into the bank and left a crescent of silty sand. "You still remember?" he asked.

I nodded. I'd just turned thirteen and, against the orders of my parents, had gone swimming there with a bunch of kids. Mike was with us and decided it was time to learn to swim. His method was to jump in and hope that his survival instinct would do the job. I'd always been strong in the water and managed to get to him before he joined the crud at the bottom of the river.

"A lot of water under the bridge since then," I said, laughing at my own wit.

Mike smiled. He tapped his bottle against mine and said, "Here's to the end of water under the bridge." I drank, but he pitched his bottle out into the river, beer spraying in a foamy arc, like a shooting star in the middle of the day.

Nash and Scottie weren't related, but you would have thought they were brothers the way they stuck together on everything. It was common gossip on the base that their dads were piss tanks, which was something, since drinking was the number one recreational pastime for pretty well every adult I knew. I'd once heard a rumour that Nash's old man was seen kissing Scottie's mom, his hand up her shirt, in the garage at one of their rowdy barbecues. Whether it was true or not, the two dads were still friends, and their sons seemed to be trying to live up to their parents' reputations. If there was a party anywhere within fifty miles of us, Nash and Scottie knew about it.

So it was no big surprise when they told Gwyn and me about the beach social out at Norquay Lake. "There's even going to be a band in the pavilion: The Demons," Scottie said.

"The Demons?" I said. "You want to party with those greasers?"

"Greaser band means greaser chicks," Nash said, leering. "And you know what they're like. Scottie's looking for some action." He punched Scottie in the arm and the two laughed like a couple of pimply-faced howler monkeys.

"Oops, sorry, Wheeler," Scottie said, as if he'd suddenly remembered Gwyn was sitting beside me. "We forgot you're married."

"We're not married, you goon," she said. She shook her head. "Sometimes you guys are such teenagers." She said it as if being a teenager were something to strive to overcome. But this comment on the state of their maturity only made them cackle more.

Gwyn wasn't usually interested in parties, especially not the sort that attracted Nash and Scottie. But for some reason I felt I should assert myself. "Okay, we'll go."

She looked at me. "Wheeler," she said; nothing else.

"The only problem is getting a ride out there," Nash said. The lake was about fifteen miles east of town.

"Don't worry," I answered. "Mike's got a car. I'll get him to take us."

"That Mousie guy?" Scottie asked.

"I don't recommend you calling him that," I said, but I wasn't sure who would win a duke-out between the two of them. And I also wasn't certain the ride was in the bag. I hadn't seen Mike for weeks, since the day we'd gone to the bridge.

Later, I walked Gwyn home the long way, around the playing fields where the branches of bordering willows hung to the ground and offered some privacy. I put my arm around her waist and leaned in to kiss her on the neck. She pushed me away. "What's wrong with you?" I said.

"I don't want to go."

"To the party? Why not? Let's do something interesting for a change."

She stopped walking. "Are you saying that being with me is boring?"

The sun through the leaves washed over her like underwater light, and I wanted to kiss the soft skin along her cheek. "Of course not," I said. "But what's the big deal about going to a beach party?"

Gwyn walked away from me with her arms crossed in front of her. She looked comical, and for a moment I thought I might start laughing. But I choked it back and kept a neutral expression on my face.

"You know," she said, "you're so used to getting your own way, you don't even realize there might be another side to things."

I had no idea what she was talking about, but I began to feel almost bloated with determination to go to that party. "It'll be fun," I said. "You'll see. And if it isn't, we'll leave early."

I called Mike and convinced him to drive us to Norquay when he finished work on Friday. I promised him we'd pay for gas and beer. "And there'll be women all over the place," I said. "Maybe you'll get lucky."

"If I do, how are you going to get home?" he asked.

I had to go through all the pockets in my parents' closet to scrape up enough money for my share, but getting the beer was easy. Scottie's older brother would buy it for us if we threw in enough extra to cover a mickey of rye for him.

We met Mike in the skating rink parking lot. Scottie was sitting on the beer, which was covered by his jacket, when Mike pulled into the gravelled lot. He'd washed and polished his car, and cleaned the interior.

"Let's get this in the trunk, before the SPs come around to check us out," Scottie said, standing, the wrapped boxes looking obvious under his arm.

After Mike unlocked the trunk, he came around and opened the front passenger door. "All aboard," he said, and waved Gwyn into the car. I climbed in beside her and the other two got into the back.

Once we were moving, Nash offered around a flask of what he called "cocktail"—a disgusting but potent mix from the stock in his old man's liquor cabinet. "He knows exactly how much is in each bottle," Nash said. His dad may have been heavy into the booze, but he wasn't stupid. "It takes forever to get enough to drink because I can only take a few drops at a time."

"Pure stealth," Scottie said.

"Persistence," I countered.

"Lack of anything useful to do," Gwyn said. Mike laughed at this, and from the corner of my eye, I could see Scottie giving Mike the finger and mouthing the name "Mousie."

Normally, Gwyn didn't drink, but when Mike handed her the bottle, she took a sip and almost spit it right back out. I howled and patted her on the back. Mike gave her a piece of gum to get the taste out of her mouth.

By the time we got to the lake, the party had shifted into its second stage. The teenyboppers had gone home and those who were left, or were still arriving, were the more serious partiers. The Demons had set up on the park bandstand, and down on the beach a bunch of kids from North Side were piling up wood from the campsite area for a bonfire.

North Side was widely acknowledged as the poorest and meanest part of town. On the base, anyone from there was considered a greaser and potential trouble. Likewise, they generally hated air force kids. I tried to avoid them whenever possible, especially on an occasion like this. But Scottie and Nash went right over and started to help gather firewood. Mike, Gwyn and I sat at a picnic table and watched the progress of the bonfire. I thought Scottie was crazy, wading in among the black leather and Levis, wearing his green and white jacket with Air Marshall Curtis School across its back.

"Now this isn't so bad, is it?" I said to Gwyn, then turned to Mike. "She didn't want to come, but I talked her into it."

"I don't have much fun at parties," she said.

"I know what you mean," Mike said. "Somebody usually does something really stupid and everyone around them pays the price."

"Hey," I said. "Thanks for the back-up." Mike shrugged. I could see Scottie and Nash were already talking to some girls. Nash got out his flask, took a drink and passed it to a tall girl with bleached hair and a red Mackinaw.

The night sky was lit up by the bonfire, and glowing red embers drifted high into the air around us. We could hear The Demons over in the pavilion, grinding through their version of "Let's Dance." All around, drunken teenagers crashed through the bush or sat on the beach in amorous embraces. I had just finished my third beer when Gwyn said she wanted to go.

"Now?" I asked.

"Why not? You said we could leave early."

I started to look to Mike, then doubted he'd support me in declaring her request unreasonable. "Well, do you want to try to convince Scottie and Nash?"

"I should have known," she said, and got up from the table.

"Where are you going?" I shouted.

"For a walk."

"Goddamn it," I said and was about to give Mike shit for taking her side earlier, when Nash came running up, waving his arms and calling our names.

Nash's glasses were twisted and so far off kilter I wanted to laugh, but the look on his face ruled out that response. "Scottie's in deep shit," he said. "Some North Side greaser said he was putting moves on his chick. Now there's five of them and they want to fight. Come on." Nash turned and ran back down the path that led through the trees to the bandstand.

I didn't like the situation, but I felt secure with Mike there. At least some of the North Siders would know who he was and would be wary of him. Mike shook his head and said, "It's his fight, Wheeler, it's what he wants. Let him have it." Then he turned around and walked away.

"Hurry the fuck up, you guys," Nash called. He hadn't seen Mike go. My heart wasn't in Scottie's confrontation, but I didn't want to be known as someone who abandoned his friends. I wasn't sure what to do. It was as if I'd paused midstep and for the first time had to think about where my foot was going to come down. I could see Mike join Gwyn on the other side of the fire, could see them talking. Behind me, Nash kept shouting for me to hurry. My mouth was dry and my head felt weightless.

I took another look at Mike and Gwyn, then headed down the path where Nash had disappeared. As I got closer to the pavilion, the music grew louder and the glow from the stage leached through the leaves and branches. I wondered if I would regret this decision and though I didn't want to think about it, considered the many ways I might end up wishing I'd done things differently.

In the parking area behind the pavilion, a large circle of spectators had already formed. That was where I aimed myself. "Hey," I shouted, then louder, "Hey." My voice sounded clear to me, much more certain than I felt. The sky was black and I couldn't see the stars because of the stage lights and I knew then that many things were about to change, but for the moment, I simply didn't care.

Paper Covers Rock

Dugg drove like a man with his hair on fire, she thought—all morning, since they'd left the HiWay Inn outside Regina with a bogus credit-card payment. Only a week had passed since he first sat beside her at Tim Hortons back in Thunder Bay. "Sprinkles," Dugg had said, nodding toward her multicoloured doughnut. He handed her a chocolate honey-glaze, as if it were a sacrament. "Try this." And she'd bit. Now she was riding shotgun into her future.

"Hand me the pipe and take the wheel," he said, red-rimmed eyes rolling around his head like pebbles in a jar.

"Kiss my candy apple," she answered. "I'm not driving. I don't like the concept of all that responsibility." Her short plaid skirt over ragged denim jeans. Electric blue bowler's jacket with a name patch on the arm: "Suze."

"Suze," he said. "Don't break my trust, don't bring me down, just plain don't." He swung into a crescent of gravel at the road edge, raising a cloud of sand and grit that backwashed across the Cherokee. As the dust storm settled over the jeep, he was already tamping a serious pinch of Alaskan thunderfuck tight into the bowl of the water pipe.

"Suze?" she said, then remembered the jacket. "Right. Cool—Suze. But don't ask me to drive."

Dugg gestured to the book of matches on the dash. "Come on baby, light my fire."

"Retro," she said, but took the hint and sparked his hit, then had another turn herself. "Welcome to our road movie," she hissed, letting the smoke out and sputtering into a long giggle.

Dugg laughed, too, but into the pipe, which caused ember and ash from the bowl to explode across the front of his vintage Michael Jackson T-shirt and onto his lap. "Shit," he said, slapping and rubbing at himself, which sent Suze up another notch on the laugh-o-metre.

"Shut up," he snarled.

She could see he was in no mood for humour. His mean spirit ice-aged her momentum, and she sank into herself, arms folded tight across her chest. Outside, prairie wind scattered and reassembled meagre snow dunes over brown stubble fields. "Fucking winter," she said. "I hate winter."

"If you say that one more time, I'm gonna turn this sucker around and return it to its rightful owner, whoever that may be: doctor, lawyer or candlestick maker."

"Yeah right," she answered without looking at him. "I'm sure he'll be thank-you all over."

As he drove back onto the highway, Dugg smiled. "Nothing can stop a rock rolling downhill."

All it takes is movement to make him happy, she thought. "I have to pee," she said. "And I'm getting hungry."

Dugg read the green and white sign as they passed it: "Fisher—14 kay-ems. We can stop there—they must have a 7-Eleven. Maybe sell some of that worthless homegrown to the locals."

Already, she had lost her taste for Pringles and Zero bars and triangular wedges of sandwich wrapped in cellophane. "Couldn't we look for a Burger King or something?" she asked.

"Look," he said. "Do you want to make it to California?" She nodded. "Then quit whining. Unless you've figured out how to rip off a Whopper and a side of fries."

At least he's not a major creep, she kept reminding herself. At least. That's what she was thinking when they hit the coyote. It looked like somebody's dog running up out of the ditch in front of them and even she could see there was no way to miss it. Whump.

"Christ all—" he said, and had enough sense to ease on the brakes.

"Back up," she said, twisting around in her seat.

When he stopped the jeep, she jumped out and ran down to where the animal lay on a skiff of snow. It reminded her of an old blanket, thrown away in a heap. She knelt there and put her hand on the rough fur of its chest, felt the rack of rib bones, a movement of breath. "It's a coyote," she said. "Still alive." She slid her arms underneath, tried to lift. "Help me get it into the car."

"Hey," he said. "It's probably got fleas and stuff. I don't think it's a good idea."

But she was already standing, the limp body lighter than it looked, the way wild things are. "Open the back door," she said.

She placed the animal on the seat, then climbed in beside it. "We'll have to take it to a vet," she said.

"Are you nuts?" he shouted. "What are we going to pay a vet with? A bag of pot?"

"Use the credit card."

"We already used it too many times. I threw it out the window thirty miles ago. Look, it's either the dog or the coast—what do you want?"

"It's not a dog, it's a coyote," she said.

"Dog, coyote, timber wolf. Whatever." She watched him circle the jeep, cursing and kicking at the gravel shoulder. He came back to the open door. "All right," he said. "But I'm going to have to make a sale first." He reached past her into the black sport bag, dug around for a few tightly rolled baggies. "I get hungry, too, you know." She touched his arm and when he looked up at her, she smiled.

She gently stroked the animal's neck and stared at the two long-haired greasers crammed into the front with Dugg. Wearing jeans and Mackinaws, the pair matched a billion guys she'd known back home. Probably metalheads, she thought, think they're special because they can drink a case of beer and still air guitar through Megadeth's latest. The one who called himself Snake had laughed when Dugg asked for directions to the vet's. "For a fucking coyote?" he said, looking into the back seat. She watched the cold sore on his upper lip crack with his sneer, and hoped it hurt.

"Hey, dude," Dugg said. "It's got a right to live, too." The big one, Randy, told Dugg to drive around behind the derelict Texaco on the town's western edge.

They parked with the engine running and Dugg lit up a joint thin as pencil lead. She knew it was the quality stuff, unlike that in the baggies. "Good shit," Randy said. Snake nodded as he inhaled.

Dugg reached into his jacket and pulled out three bags.

"Interested?" he asked.

Randy grabbed all three and stuffed them into his jean pockets. "Let's go, Snake," he said, and they got out of the jeep.

For a moment, Dugg seemed paralyzed with surprise. Then he jumped out and went after them, almost skating on the icy lot. "Hey you buttholes—either pay for that or give it back."

They stopped and let him catch up. "Or what?" Snake said. "You gonna go tell the Mounties some guys took your drugs?"

Randy gave Dugg a push, and she watched as he fell, trying to keep his footing. She slid a bit herself on the way to where he lay, holding his wrist and howling. "You jerks," she shouted. "You're nothing." Without turning, Randy waved the three bags above his head.

"Jesus," Dugg moaned, "I think it's broken."

She drove, reluctant but careful, back to the 7-Eleven. The clerk, a tall thin redhead who reminded her of her best friend from elementary school, explained where the clinic was and told her the vet's was in Solderville, about five minutes north. She stared into the girl's pale blue eyes, then asked, "Your name's not Ruth, by any chance?"

She brought a cup of water for the coyote—spilled a little on its long pink tongue and the animal licked its muzzle. A good sign, she thought. When they got to the clinic, she told Dugg to sit down, then explained his situation to the receptionist, handing over his Ontario health card.

"Wait here," she told Dugg. "I'll be back."

For the first time, she saw uncertainty in his eyes. "Suze," he asked. "Where are you going?"

"To the vet," she said. "Look, it's a wild animal. Maybe he won't ask for money. Anyway, I'm taking it there."

"You aren't planning to ditch me here, are you?"

"I thought about it," she said. She glanced around the room, at the chrome and orange vinyl chairs, and a framed print of mountains somewhere, a lake. Then she bent to kiss the top of his head and walked out into the brilliant cold.

So Great to be Alive

From where I sit, I can see over bougainvillea and across wide lawns to the ships floating in a motionless haze on Manila Bay. Seven-thirty in the morning and already the sun is working spikey-hot fingers into my shoulders. The warmth feels good—far away from winter in Kyoto. I couldn't take another day of teaching English to a roomful of twelve-year-old Japanese girls who giggled whenever I asked them a question. Other than that, I don't know exactly why I'm here. The Philippines was never a place high on my list of must-see destinations. Maybe it's the way Rachel always talked as if her trip here had been a few months of heaven on earth. Ironic that I'm alone on a concrete bench in Rizal Park, and she's tanning on some beach in Bali or wandering among Thai hill-tribe people with that Israeli guy, Yakob.

"They'd eat you alive," she'd said, laughing, teasing me when I'd expressed an interest in travelling there.

The park is active for so early in the day, although there are two other men sitting separate and silent on benches next to mine. Couples and families stroll the walkways as if it's Sunday afternoon. And a gang of kids in ragged shirts and shorts keeps running past me, laughing, shouting and chasing each other. I turn a bit, and prop my feet up on top of my backpack; I have a feeling I should keep some physical contact with it.

Half the passengers on the bargain charter flight from Tokyo were Japanese businessmen—probably one of those sex tours. The customs people seemed anxious to harass them, but after a quick look at my Canadian passport and visa, waved me through. I breezed out the main doors and into a mob of taxi drivers, each insisting there was no other or no more reliable transportation. But I pleased myself by finding a public bus to the city for only three pesos—a tenth of the taxi fare. Now, I'm in no hurry. The tourist information office likely won't open for a while, so I lean back to enjoy the scenery.

Off to my left, I notice three young guys with cameras around their necks and blue vests with gold stitching that says "Rizal Park Photographer." This trio is standing around a fire in an oil barrel, tossing bits of trash into it. The way they keep looking at me, I have no doubt I'm the topic of conversation. Then, as if something has been decided among them, one of the three walks over to my bench. He's short and slim with a crescent smile and dark eyes that scan me like a banker sizing up a client. Above his eyebrow a lump of flesh the size of a hazelnut pokes out from the hair combed over his forehead. "Good morning, sir," he says. "I wonder if you would like a souvenir photo of yourself in our beautiful park?"

"No thanks," I answer. I give him my best polite, dismissive smile and turn away.

"No? Okay, all right," he says, then moves around the bench to face me. "By the way, my name is Rocky."

"Like the squirrel?"

Rocky looks puzzled. "No. Like in the American movies. Rocky." He takes a pack of Broadway cigarettes from his vest pocket, expertly taps one halfway out and offers it. I shake my head and he puts them away without lighting one for himself. "Have you visited Manila before?"

"Nope. This is my first time."

Rocky sits on the bench beside me. A small red and black insect crawls across the space between us. "Then you will need a room," he says, reaching out to squash the insect with the side of his thumb, then brushing it off against the edge of the bench. "Some hotels here are not safe. My friend has a very good hotel. Of course, he likes foreigners. I can arrange for you to stay there. He will give you the best discount price." Rocky reaches for my pack. "Okay, come on with me. We can take a taxi there now."

I pull the pack aside and stand up. I'm not particularly big, but I'm about half a head taller than him. "No," I say. "I don't think so, Rocky. I don't think we'll be going anywhere."

Rocky looks at me for a moment, then shrugs. "Okay, sir," he says, "no photo, no hotel. Okay." He turns and walks back to his pals, who've been watching. One of them speaks and Rocky's reply, whatever it is, makes them laugh.

Since I'm already on my feet, and I no longer feel comfortable in the park, I decide to look for the tourist information centre. I stop a man in a suit, and he directs me across the avenue, where several colonial-style government buildings are horseshoed around a pool and fountain. The central ornament of the fountain is a large wrought-iron globe of the earth, succumbing to rust on every continent. Along the pool's edge sits a circle of weary-looking Filipinos—children and adults—some splashing water on their faces, scrubbing hands.

I get the feeling they live in the park and remember Rachel saying Manila was the saddest place she'd ever been. Her face had gone dark for a moment, but then she started talking about the great snorkelling off somewhere called Puerto Gallero, and she brightened again.

When I find the tourist bureau, the door is locked behind a heavy gate.

According to the sign, it won't be open for another hour, so I go back to the fountain and sit next to a girl who looks about ten years old. She's sharing a bread roll with a younger boy. She glances at me, a friendly glance, then turns back to the boy. The boy is dressed in a T-shirt and shorts, like the kids I'd seen earlier, and the girl is wearing a faded, patterned jumper. She tears what's left of the roll into two pieces, hands him one and finishes hers before turning toward me.

"Hello," she says, her little face dirty and much too worn-out for a child's. "What country do you come from?" she asks.

"Canada." I make an obviously mock solemn face. "And what country are you from?"

She laughs and says, "I'm from the Philippines, of course. My name is Kettie and this is my brother, Thomas." I wave at Thomas, who regards me shyly. "What's your name?" she asks.

I look from side to side, then put my finger to my lips. "It's a secret," I say. I'm not sure why, but I don't want to tell them my name. Maybe it's because of the exchange I've just had with Rocky, maybe it's just something in the air here.

Kettie waits a moment, then turns to Thomas. "Say 'good morning' to Mr. Secret."

Thomas is obedient and says softly, "Good morning, Mr. Secret."

Kettie looks at my backpack and asks, "Are you looking for a room?"

"Yes. But I'll have to wait for the tourist office to open."

"We can take you to a hotel. A good place for tourists—clean and not far away," she says.

"That's okay," I say. "I don't mind waiting. It's only an hour."

Kettie stands. "Who knows if it will be open at all today?" she says. "Mr. Secret, I know a good hotel for you. Thomas and I will show you the way. You don't have to give us any money." I realize she's trying to make me understand she genuinely doesn't want anything from me. Around the pool people are still washing or eating, a few of them watching us. "Okay," I say. "Lead on."

We pass the modern Western hotels with their sweeping palm trees, tidily gardened entrances and armed doormen, into the Ermita district. Here, women holding babies have staked out most of the sidewalk with large, flat baskets of peanuts and bunches of stunted bananas. Humid air mixes the fragrances of frying fish, wood smoke and rot with the petitions of beggars and sellers, the noise of traffic.

From just behind me a harsh car-horn version of "La Cucaracha" forces me up off the street to avoid being hit by a Jeepney. Instead, I almost collide with two heavily made-up young women. The passenger vehicle, painted yellow, black and green, has a brilliant chrome rooster mounted on each of its front fenders. I watch the message across its back—God is Love—growing smaller as it moves down the narrow roadway. "Hello mister," one of the women speaks, and I see that underneath the blood-red lipstick and dark eyeliner, these two aren't much older than the students I'd been teaching in Japan. "Are you looking for a girlfriend?" the other asks.

"Uh, no, thank you," I answer, trying to convey in my tone that I'm not making a moral judgement on them, then wonder why this matters to me. It doesn't seem important to the girls, who simply stare.

"Come on, Mr. Secret," Kettie says, and takes my hand to lead me along. Her tiny fingers feel delicate, fragile.

Finally, near the end of a string of bars, "go-go" clubs, hotels and tourist restaurants, we arrive at the Congress Family Hotel. I find it a relief to enter the calm and quiet of its lobby. Kettie speaks in Tagalog to the old woman behind the counter, who appears suspicious of the little girl and her brother, standing silently behind her. The woman, frowning, keeps up a conversation with Kettie while she registers me. She gives me a receipt, and hands me a key from a numbered rack mounted below a dusty crucifix.

I thank Kettie and her brother, tell them that maybe I'll see them the next time I'm in Rizal Park. And, as we had arranged, I don't offer them anything for their help.

"Today is a special day, Mr. Secret," Kettie says. "There will be a free movie tonight in the park. If you come tonight, you will find us there. I hope we can meet again." I shake hands with each of them, and wave to them as they leave.

My room is on the second floor, and as I close the door, I find a list of safety instructions on the wall, including what to do in case of earthquake. At the end of the list is a polite request not to leave "valuables, guns or deadly weapons" in the room. Does that mean I'll need them on the street?

Despite the bleak list, I feel secure and pleasantly alone in this room with its barred windows. The dingy, high-ceilinged walls enclose a wardrobe, a dresser, a chair next to a small wooden table, and a metal-frame bed made up with clean, white sheets. I toss my bag on the bed and begin to unpack, when suddenly I realize I haven't eaten anything—except a plasticky airline snack—since supper last night.

Outside the hotel, I'm not sure where to go. But across the street, a tall black man is talking to one of the women selling fruit. He's wearing a white shirt and carrying a leather shoulder bag, and looks like he might be an American serviceman.

"Excuse me," I say. "I wonder if you know of a decent restaurant around here—not too expensive?"

He seems startled at first, then relaxes and answers. "Let me think—well, the Kangaroo Klub is nearby. It's reasonable." His speech is slow and careful, as if I've posed a tough question. Suddenly, he looks at me as if he'd just noticed me. "As I'm not busy right now, let me show you where it is."

On the way he introduces himself as Amos Hummingbird, and says he's a nightclub entertainer. "That's why I dress this way," he says, and gestures at the sharply creased brown slacks and the almost luminous shirt. "When I walk into a club, I have to be better dressed than the boss." He claims he's an American but was born in Trinidad. I tell him my name is Mr. Secret. It feels a bit goofy, but I look him in the face as I speak, and he seems to accept it.

The Kangaroo Klub turns out to be a combination travel agency/social centre run mainly for Australians. I'm a bit surprised when Amos doesn't leave me at the entrance, but leads the way inside. He sits across from me at one of several mismatched chrome and vinyl dining sets, apparently resurrected from the late 1950s. Clearly, he isn't going anywhere, so I give in.

"Can I buy you a coffee?" I ask.

"No, thank you. Coffee is too hard on the insides. But I would like some soup." Before I can react, Amos looks up and shouts to the waitress. "Honey, bring me a bowl of beef soup. And a roll, and a glass of milk."

The waitress comes to the table with a small basket of bread, and takes my order for an omelette and coffee.

"Thank you kindly, for buying me lunch," he says. "A man feels revived when his belly is full. Obviously, you are a generous man, considerate of others, unlike some people in this town."

Since I know the meal won't cost much, and this development is right in line with the sequence of events that's so far been my introduction to Manila, I resign myself to paying.

Meanwhile, Amos keeps up a monologue about how hard it is to find work in this town. "I left the States three years ago," he says, "with a contract to perform in Tokyo. From there I went on to Taipei, Seoul, Bangkok, Singapore and eventually wound up here." As he speaks, I form a mental image of Amos's career slowly spiralling outward, drifting farther and farther from centre. Amos's peak, his ultimate achievement, had been to play as Rochester with Jack Benny for one week in Hong Kong.

"Mr. Benny was a great entertainer," Amos says. He looks hard into my eyes, as if daring me to disagree. "A real gentleman. Each night after the show, he took me to dinner at his own expense."

The wall next to us is a lattice of split bamboo. Through its spaces, I can see a group of kids watching us. As soon as they notice me looking at them, they rush toward us. One of the bigger ones puts his hand through the lattice and says, "Peso, mister? Please, mister." But instead of money, I give him one of the rolls from the basket. Suddenly there are hands coming through the wall like something from a bad horror movie. I quickly pass out the bread, and when it's gone I wave the waitress over and point at the basket, saying, "More bread, please—put it on my bill." She brings the rolls but before I can hand them all out, someone from the restaurant comes around the corner outside, shouting in Tagalog, and the kids take off. I look at Amos, who, throughout, has just been watching me.

When the waitress brings our food, Amos and I both eat ferociously. He finishes his meal first, sets his spoon down gently and wipes his mouth with his napkin. "What would you say is the greatest invention of the human race?" he asks.

"I don't know—the wheel?"

"Cremation," he says.

I start to grin, then glance up and realize he's serious. "How do you mean that?" I say.

"Have you ever heard of catalepsy?" he asks. "It's a paralysis of the body, sometimes mistaken for death. In fact, it's more common than most people realize. I've made a careful study of the subject." He leans closer and drops his voice to a whisper; I notice a line of sweat forming along his upper lip. "My greatest fear is to be buried alive. That's why I'm in favour of cremation. Can you imagine what it would be like to wake up and find yourself in a coffin, six feet under the ground? Alive but as good as dead?" Amos shudders unself-consciously.

"I have to get out of this city," he says. "Manila isn't good for me." Amos begins tapping his spoon against his empty glass. "A friend once lent me $200, no questions asked. He saw that I needed the money and he knew he would get it all back. Within six months, I repaid every penny. If I only knew where that man was now, I would contact him immediately."

I understand that I'm being asked to take the place of the missing friend, but I don't say a word, only nod sympathetically.

Eventually, Amos speaks, his voice returned to its former tone as if we'd been chatting about the quality of the meal. "Well, I believe I ought to be going," he says.

"I should get moving, too," I say, and leave a few coins on the table as a tip. I notice Amos look at them, then quickly glance away, and we walk outside together. The kids and the bread are long gone.

I decline Amos's offer to take me sightseeing; tell him I have to return to my hotel. In the room, I stretch out on the bed, keeping close to the edge where the sag is least noticeable, thinking about catalepsy and being buried alive and Amos Hummingbird stuck in Manila. I recall a cartoon Rachel once showed me: two tired-looking guys with briefcases are walking down a residential street on a sunny afternoon. One says to the other, "You know, it's days like this that make you wish you were alive."

When I wake, it's dark and I feel disoriented, uncertain of where I am. The stillness of the room seems unnatural when I can sense movement and activity outside, hear its muted drone. As my thoughts fall back into place, I'm surprised that I've slept so long and so deeply. In the washroom, I splash cold water on my face, but I still feel groggy. I change into a clean shirt from my suitcase, then lock the door behind me and start out for Rizal Park.

Most of the sidewalk vendors have left, but I find a woman who sells me a large bag of roasted peanuts, some bananas and two mangoes. I wave off the change she hands me, and she looks pleased with this end-of-day bonus.

By the time I reach the park, the movie is already in progress on a large screen constructed of what looks like several sheets of whitewashed plywood. Elvis Presley is singing and dancing his way through a film I recognize as *Viva Las Vegas*. His huge face lights up the centre of Manila, and the slightly dated glitter depicting the American dream seems grotesque. I wander through the crowd, everyone staring intently at the screen from the grass and the walkways. The benches, sidewalks and rectangles of lawn are thick with people. I step over legs, searching for the faces of Kettie and Thomas, hoping that if I don't spot them, they might notice me. But it feels hopeless. Out on the bay, the dark shapes of the ships are still visible in the moonlight, and lights flicker on a few of them. Behind me, a jubilant young Elvis rises in a helicopter above Las Vegas and the surrounding desert, and all at once, the audience begins to cheer.

Bisecting Mirror

I was drinking a long espresso in the Vienna Café when Roth brought me the news. Roth was a photographer, my closest friend at the time. He was going through a period of taking close-up portraits of everyone he knew. The day before he'd shown me a trick he did with the prints.

"Watch this," he'd said, and set a mirror down the middle of the face, vertically bisecting the image from forehead to chin. The portrait was of a woman I'd secretly been in love with for years. Beautiful, confident and focussed—the type of woman I knew would never have been interested in me. Besides, I was a married man. The new image, composed of the right side of her face in symmetry, presented her as the person I thought she was. But when he reversed the mirror so the left side of her face was duplicated, the image changed drastically. Suddenly, here was an almost timid-looking woman, someone who appeared to be harbouring a secret fear. I wondered what he'd seen when he tried this procedure on my picture, but I didn't ask.

Anyway, I was staring into my coffee, listening to Coleman Hawkins and Ben Webster playing "La Rosita" when Roth sat down across from me. Those throaty tenor saxes drifting me into a '40s film noir landscape.

"Don't count on Doctor Dave for any more paycheques," he said, excitement flashing in his eyes. "The RCMP hauled him out of his house in handcuffs last night."

Burroughs is a dentist, but Roth always calls him Doctor Dave. I'd been working for him two weeks, helping build a horse barn on his property. His girls were into horses and he usually gave them whatever they wanted. But I hadn't been paid yet and was banking on about six more weeks' work there.

"Apparently he's got another family up in Kamloops," Roth continued. "A wife and a baby. I told you he was an asshole."

"Judge not," I said, squaring up a small pile of crumbs on the table top. The music moved on to Joe Lovano doing "Love Is a Many Splendored Thing." I remembered the way Burroughs had often complained about how hard it was to meet expenses; I'd thought he was just a cheapskate. "He seemed to be around here an awful lot," I said, "what did he tell the woman in Kamloops he was doing?"

"Who knows?"

"Man, it never would have occured to me."

Roth laughed. "You didn't see his portrait," he said. At the time, I didn't realize he'd missed my meaning.

As Do the Birds

This morning I get up early and drive to the Elias Lodge, which looks down across the flats toward the Fraser River. Melanie and the baby are still asleep, so I leave a note and take an orange to eat on the way. I'm anxious to see my sister, Becky, because I have a new tape I want to play for her. In the lodge, the nurses keep everyone's door open during the day, so when I get to her room I find her sitting in her wooden rocker. As always, her thumb and finger work together as if rolling a bead between them, over and over. She is concentrating on a handful of sparrows fussing around the empty birdbath outside her window.

A scatter of bright red pyrocantha berries has fallen there and the sparrows are having a feed, watched by a pair of

Steller's jays. The jays' scruffy crests give them the appearance of needing their hair brushed, a look which reminds me of my sister. Her wild hair, greying prematurely but once so blonde it appeared almost white, reaches out in places like tendrils on a grapevine. I stand in the doorway for a moment, trying to hear what Becky is muttering. I know that as soon as she becomes aware of anyone coming near her, she'll stop talking.

"Hey," I say, "are you spying on those poor little creatures?"

Becky turns and smiles at me. "Not spying, silly brother—having a talk with them."

"What were you talking about?"

Becky pulls herself up out of the rocker and shuffles over to give me a weak hug. Once, she would have leapt out of that chair and embraced me like a drowning person grabbing a float, but that was another lifetime. As I do each time I see her, I feel amazed at how thin and brittle she's become. "They're taking turns," she says.

"Who is?"

"The sparrows and the jays. Taking turns at the berries."

"I've brought you something," I say, and wave the cassette tape in the air between us. I put the tape into the deck I bought her (like most of the other personal touches in her room) and press play, watching to see if she recognizes the music.

Well into the first chorus of "It'll Shine When it Shines," I finally speak. "Recognize this?"

"Should I?" she asks, and appears a bit worried, as if she's screwing up on some kind of quiz.

"Trout Mountain String Band," I say. "It's from the old coffee house in Quesnel. Grant, the guy who played fiddle, has a web site, so I contacted him and he sent me the tape." This is music from our past, a time we moved through long ago—a time that had its sadness but also bright happiness. I hope that hearing it might bring back something, rekindle some of her old light.

"That's a good name for a band," she says. She examines the cassette case. There's only a list of the songs, handwritten with a kind of liquid-gold pen. "Did we ever hear them, Porter?"

"Once or twice," I lie. "There's no reason for you to remember. I just thought you might."

She turns back to the window. "Look," she says, pointing, "the jays are eating now."

Even though she's a year older than me, it seems like I've been taking care of Becky all my life. There were the small things: taking the blame for her clumsiness or lack of attention, fixing things she'd broken before Dad found out. But the first time it moved outside our family was the winter I turned nine. A fierce Manitoba blizzard one night meant our school was closed the next day. Most of the kids in the neighbourhood were playing on a monstrous drift that had blown up against the railroad snow fence. I came climbing out of a tunnel and found two boys from her class holding her down, trying to shove snow inside the front of her pants. I'd never been in a real fight before, but I knew what I had to do.

The first guy I just kicked in the ribs; he let out a whoof of air and rolled off Becky, onto his back. The other one jumped up and shouted, "What did you do that for?" He was large for his age, but so was I, and I remember the astonishment on his face, as if I'd interrupted some sacred rite.

This was a farm kid named Byron Kozak, who walked two miles each morning to come to our school. Maybe his parents didn't even know the school was closed that day. He stood there a moment, his cheeks red from the cold and exertion, and a line of snot trailing down his upper lip. He was broad across the chest and had a large head with a forest of dull black hair; his nickname was Cossack. "That's my sister," I said, and nailed him right in the centre of his looming, Slavic face. My dad had told me the best way to deal with a bully was to punch him in the nose before he expected anything.

The Cossack fell, shrieking, and I wiped my fist on the snow, more worried about having his snot on my mitts than about blood. I ignored the two boys and helped Becky up from the ground. She cried all the way home, and I wondered how much of what had happened I should tell my parents.

At that time, Dad had just started work for the Co-op store outside Portage la Prairie, about fifty miles west of Winnipeg. It seemed he did a little of everything—driving truck, managing the warehouse or working the shelves in the store. Later, when I began high school, he got me a part-time job there. For a long while I resented having to spend time after school and weekends bagging and carrying groceries—none of the kids I hung out with had a job to worry about, plus I felt embarrassed by the green and white uniform I had to wear. But eventually I learned to appreciate my situation for what I gained: a knowledge of how to handle hard work, and a bank account of my own, which came in useful later.

When I was fifteen, our mom took off with a cab driver, and like in some mediocre country song, we never heard from her again. Her leaving hurt me, and I felt ashamed. I avoided my few friends, rather than take the chance they might find out. But the sadness I endured also hollowed out a space inside me I knew I could retreat to any time, a place where I could rely on myself. The loss hit Becky much harder. About two weeks after Mom left, the principal called me out of class to ask why Becky wasn't at school that day and was everything all right at home? I suspected rumours had reached him about my family's predicament and he wanted to verify them with me. I told him my sister had the flu and that I had forgotten to pass the message along to her teacher. The principal accepted my apology, but watched me carefully for a few moments before he let me return to class. I felt even more nervous and humiliated than I already was.

After school, I came home and found Becky sitting on her bed, clutching a sheet of paper. I could tell she'd been crying, although when I got there she was smiling and rocking with her eyes closed.

"Why didn't you tell me you were staying home?" I demanded. "Old man Watson hauled me out of English this morning to ask me where you were. I said you were sick, but I don't know if he believed me and now I'm probably in shit, too." I noticed she was wearing a sweater I hadn't seen for a long time, pink with a line of blue knit ducks across the front, and far too small for her.

"Mom sent me a letter," she said. Her eyes were open now, red and the eyelashes sticky-looking.

"A letter? Let me see."

"No. It's for me, not for you."

Normally I would have tried to convince her with argument and persistence, but the anger that had been building in me took over. "Give me the goddamn letter," I shouted, and grabbed for the paper. The top of the sheet tore off in my hands. Becky screamed and fought to get it back, but I easily held her away with one arm while I read what was written there: *My dear sweet Becky, my little duckling, Mama will be back soon*, unmistakably in Becky's own handwriting.

I gave her back the paper, put my arm around her and told her I was sorry for tearing her letter. As she leaned into me, sobbing and spluttering, I realized it was my second apology of the day—but this one I really meant.

Long before she left, my mom and dad had begun to avoid each other around the house. They couldn't make a decision about anything without arguing first, and eventually he set up his bedroom in the basement. He'd had an almost relieved look on his face when he told us she was gone—as if something he'd dreaded had come to pass, and had turned out not nearly as bad as he'd anticipated. "Good riddance," he'd said. And so I never would have imagined Dad would genuinely miss her. But I guess he did. He started bringing home people from the bar and partying most nights. He'd always told me to stay away from drugs, but I found roaches in the ashtray in the mornings, and once he had to call an ambulance to come get a woman who'd freaked out on LSD and locked herself in the downstairs bathroom. He woke me up to be there when the paramedics arrived. I could hear her shouting that no one should touch her. "No, no," she shrieked, like a skate blade on pavement. "It's fire; I'm burning."

"I'm a bit on edge, myself," my dad said. He wouldn't look me in the eye and kept rubbing his hands across his face. Everyone had cleared out and I sat on the couch while he paced the living room, stepping around the beer bottles and half-full glasses his guests had abandoned. I could hear the woman crashing around in the bathroom, crying about hell and fire and unforgiven sins.

The shouting made me jittery and I worried Becky might wake up—I didn't want to have to explain all this to her. "I wish that bathroom was soundproof," I said and went to the kitchen, where I found a bottle of SevenUp on the counter, opened it and returned to the couch to watch my father manoeuvre around the room.

My father was tall, and in those days a youthful-looking man with thick, sand-coloured hair—sometimes his coworkers joked and called him "Surfer Boy"—but I noticed that night how his clothes were beginning to hang on him, and that he had a cut on his ear. No one would mistake him for a surfer boy now, I thought.

When the paramedics finally talked the screamer out of the

bathroom, I recognized her as a senior-year girl from the high school, who also worked weekends as a cashier in the store. Her uncle was an assistant manager at the Co-op; I wondered how this was going to play out for Dad.

On Monday afternoon when I got to the store, Dad was waiting for me in our Impala station wagon near the store entrance. He hit the horn lightly and waved me over.

"What's up?" I said, although I was pretty certain I could guess what had happened. All day at school, people had been pointing at me and laughing.

"We're no longer working for these pricks," he said. "Get in the car."

"We? Why should I lose my job for something you've done?" The irony of my being upset over not having to work was apparent to both of us, and in better times we would have laughed about it.

"Don't smart-mouth me," he said. He looked up into my eyes. "I told them that if they didn't want me around the store any more, then my son wouldn't be working there, either." He seemed to need something from me at that moment, but I couldn't give it to him.

I glanced at the store to see if anyone was watching, but couldn't see through the reflections in the glass. "Thanks a lot," I said.

He turned to face straight ahead and sighed. "Do you want a ride home, or do you want to walk?"

"I think I'd like to walk."

"Fine. Have it your way," he said, and put the car into gear. "Don't be late for supper."

As I trudged across the parking lot I wanted to run after him and shout in his face: "Have it my way? When the hell has it ever been my way?"

We moved to Winnipeg about a month later and lived with Dad's sister Hannah until we could afford our own place. Uncle Bernie got Dad hired as a janitor at the Boeing plant and I eventually found weekend work at a Texaco gas station. Dad settled into a more stable routine, and our family life began to move slightly back towards normal. We didn't talk about Mom, didn't even mention her if we could avoid the topic. Becky appeared to be coping with all the changes, but she insisted on leaving school and getting a job. I tried to talk her out of it; at this point we were in the same grade, and I thought we would graduate together. I gave her the standard argument: If you don't finish high school, you'll never amount to much.

She laughed and pinched my ear. "Porter, do you honestly think I'm going to pass Grade 12 and get a big-time career?" she said. I'd never heard her suggest, even tangentially, that she was aware of being what we called at the time "a little slow."

I squirmed away from her and rubbed the spot where she'd grabbed me. "Well, if you drop out now, you'll never know."

We were sitting outside on the porch of our half of the two-bedroom duplex we rented. Spring had come early that year, and though it was early April, all around us snow was melting, water running. We could hear it day and night as if we were living beside a stream. Becky wore work boots and a long, embroidered dress under her blue down-filled jacket.

"A girl in my class—Tree—told me she likes my spirit," she said. She was still smiling, but I could hear the seriousness in her voice, so I didn't challenge her. I knew who Tree was: Alicia Bowman, one of the hippie kids. "She says she can get me a job as a waitress where she works."

I realized Becky was waiting for me to give her my approval and suddenly felt the weight of this responsibility. I chipped a hunk of melting ice off the steps and tossed it into a puddle at the bottom of the stairs. "What the hell," I said. "Go ahead, if that's what you want."

She stamped her feet and squealed happily, then hugged me. "Just wait and see," she said. "I'll be the best waitress in Winnipeg."

It's amazing how, even for people with few skills at organization or planning—not so unusual for teenagers, I suppose—life can reveal its own levels of order. And not always pleasantly.

Becky got the job she wanted at the restaurant, optimistically named Over the Rainbow, which specialized in the wretched high-fibre, low-taste health-food dishes of the era. But even in this laid-back place, she was hopeless. She often forgot people's orders by the time she got to the kitchen, or mixed up bills from different tables. Finally, some love-generation entrepreneur complained when she couldn't find the cream and stirred yogurt into his chicory-root coffee, so the owners of the place moved her to bussing tables and washing dishes.

I'd seen Becky's attempts at these tasks around our house over the years and wasn't surprised when they finally laid her off because she broke too many dishes. "At least I can collect unemployment insurance," she said, "until I find something else." But I sensed she was diminished somehow by this new failure. It was one thing to screw up at home, but being fired from her job for what could only be described as incompetence did serious damage to her self-esteem. And of course she hadn't put in enough time on the job to be eligible for UI, so once again she had to rely on Dad and me.

By June the air was already full of summer and I had decided to ask my boss if he'd take me on as an apprentice mechanic once school finished. Then one Friday afternoon I cut my last class to go home early. Someone had parked a white Dodge van with Canadian flag curtains and a "High Times" bumper sticker in the driveway behind the Impala. I could hear the stereo playing "Gimme Shelter" from two houses away, and when I opened the door, my dad was right there, as if he'd been waiting for me. His eyes shone like river stones and his breath was yeasty.

"Hey, Porter," he said. "Some of Becky's friends dropped over."

Tree was sitting on the floor by the stereo, rolling a joint. Her long dark hair hung down over the shoulders of her embroidered peasant dress. Two guys I didn't recognize, wearing wide-flare bell-bottoms and plaid shirts, perched on the couch, drinking beer and watching her.

I asked, "Where's Becky?"

"She's not home yet," Dad said. "Know everybody? Want a beer?"

"Tree," I said, and she nodded. I introduced myself to Robbie and Cal, and asked my dad to come have a look at something in the kitchen. Not very subtle, I guess, but I didn't care.

Dad walked past me to the fridge. "The guys just got back from Montreal and brought a case of Moosehead with them. Want one?"

"No thanks," I said. I didn't ask what else they'd brought. "And aren't you working tonight?"

"Fuck it," he answered, holding the fridge door open, the light from inside shining through a wall of brown glass. "I'll call in sick."

"Do you think this is a smart idea?" I waved my arm back toward the living room.

"Don't get so uptight," he said. "Why can't you just go with the flow once in a while?"

I looked at him and saw the terminal shreds of the aging Surfer Boy. "So that's what you think you're doing."

I intercepted Becky at the end of the block to tell her Dad wouldn't be home for dinner and that I would treat her to spaghetti at the Roma. She let me be quiet as we walked along; she always accepted my moods. But I wasn't brooding so much as planning, going with the flow, riding air currents. The more I thought, the more the world bloomed with possibility. By the time we ordered our pasta, I had already mapped out the beginnings of the next stage of our lives.

The day after I finished high school we caught the bus to Edmonton. I'd given up on the mechanic idea, feeling instead the urge to move across a large chunk of geography.

It was almost three years later, another spring, that we landed in Quesnel in the middle of British Columbia. Becky and I moved temporarily into a miner's canvas tent beside the Fraser River among the ruins of what had once been someone's intention to create a resort, and was now called "The Sanctuary." The tent sat inside the oval of an overgrown horse-racing track. In among the barns and the four cabins, a crumbling swimming pool had been converted into a greenhouse. A bunch of cowboy-hat-wearing urban refugees lived in the cabins with their children and dogs.

We'd met one of the Sanctuary residents—Hugh, a short, bearded man with gold-capped teeth—in the Billy Barker pub. If anyone served as the centre of the group, it was Hugh. When we bumped into him, he was preparing for his summer work as a guide and outfitter in the Kluane.

"Mostly Americans with lots of money," he explained. "Trying to blow the legs out from under a Dall ram. Work my ass off all summer and capital-R relax all winter—as a system, it's been good to me for about six years now." He set his empty bottle on the terry-cloth-covered table; looked me and Becky over. "Our cabin will be empty in a few weeks," he said, gesturing to his morose-looking pal, Smiley, who nodded in agreement. Smiley had the blue L-O-V-E / H-A-T-E knuckle tattoos I'd seen on a couple other guys who'd spent time in prison. "You can stay there as long as you need to or until we're back in October, whichever comes first."

Hugh explained that the Sanctuary occupied a small corner of the Pine Ridge Ranch, which belonged to Arne Pederson. Pederson, retired now, had arrived in Quesnel in the mid-thirties with a lunch box and a bow saw. By the time we showed up, he owned the ranch, a sawmill and a logging operation.

I asked Hugh who to see at the mill to get hired. "Probably start you out on the green chain, which is hard-sweat labour," he said. "Lumber coming at you like popcorn in a windstorm."

Later, I bought a dove-grey Stetson in the town's only tack shop. I could tell that the clerk, a young woman wearing a pearl-button shirt tight across her chest, thought Becky and I were a couple, so I made a point of calling her "my sister." As I walked out into the light of day wearing the hat, Becky laughed and called me Clint Eastwood. I turned around to give her my version of the actor's trademark squint and found myself looking into a wide face framed with black hair. The way this guy stared at Becky confused me at first, then I felt a flicker of something like déja vu. "Cossack?" I said.

He glanced at me and smiled. "Nobody calls me that no more. It's Byron now." He then turned back to face my sister. "Becky Francis, right?"

Becky grinned. "I remember you, Byron Kozak. The only kid in Grade 6 who spelled worse than me."

"I was watching you talk to Hugh back in the pub," he said. "It took me a while to figure out why you looked so familiar."

"Why didn't you come over and say 'hi'?" she asked.

Byron scratched under his chin. "I don't feel real comfortable around them people. And by the way, the mill ain't hiring these days; they're laying off a shift."

"Nothing wrong with your hearing," I said.

He shrugged. "But the ranch ..." he said. Again, he looked at Becky. "I'm the lead hand there, and my partner quit two weeks ago. Know anybody who's looking for work and might be able to hack ranching?"

After that day years earlier on the snow hill, the Cossack had stayed away from me and had gradually drifted out of my thoughts. At first I'd imagined he was afraid of me, then realized he probably just found me unpredictable. Now he was sideways offering me a chance to work with him. But I could see from the kind of attention he gave Becky it wasn't me he wanted around. At that moment, I wasn't sure I liked him any more than I ever had, or that I could get comfortable with the notion of him and my sister together in any fashion, but I decided to take advantage of this opportunity, and deal with the consequences later.

Our lives quickly took on a new texture. When Hugh and Smiley went north, Becky and I moved into their three-room cabin. Each workday morning, Byron swung by in his Dodge four-by-four pickup. Most days he got there early enough to have a cup of coffee before we left. Then he and I climbed into the truck—I usually had to clear a tool box or a roll of binder twine off the seat before I could sit down—and we bounced down the old logging road to the ranch. Other than the junk Byron kept in the cab, the only thing personal about the truck was the bottle opener he'd mounted on the dash. "Standard equipment here in the Cariboo," he said.

In the cabin, Hugh had left two shelves of reading material—mostly novels and old school texts. But the books that caught Becky's attention were the ones on nature: a guide to trees and shrubs in BC, photobooks of mountains and shorelines, and a couple of field guides to birds and animals.

During the days, she struggled through these and explored the second-growth forest, the riverbank and grassy meadows, discovering wild strawberries or tender clusters of cress, which she brought back for our supper. Suddenly she was learning things about the world that neither of us had ever known. The kids who could walk and weren't in school followed her up the deer trails and across tangled, grown-over deadfall in the old logging sites. Occasionally she earned a few dollars babysitting while one or more of the mothers went into town. At night, we sat outside on the porch and she pointed out star clusters or explained the diving buzz of nighthawks in the throes of bird courtship.

Sometimes Byron joined us. One evening Becky led him down to the river to show him the place she'd seen a kingfisher disappear into a burrow in the sandy bank where it had laid its eggs. On the way, she stopped to tell him something, waving downstream toward the lights of Quesnel. I could see she was excited and wondered if she noticed that, despite whatever she was talking about, Byron simply stared into her face. After a while, she took his hand and they moved out of sight down the path.

Those days, I watched Byron carefully: studied his gestures, his attitudes, and followed his instructions, gradually beginning to feel comfortable in my role as ranch hand. When the cows started calving, he taught me to notice which mothers-to-be were missing from the early feeding, and of those, which were inexperienced and might have some trouble giving birth. This is what took me out into the northeast corner of the ranch one day and led me around a clump of scrub brush to find a three-year-old cow lying in the dirt with one hoof and part of the head of a calf protruding from her hind end. Her tongue spilled from her mouth like a wet sock and her eyes were filled with a frantic terror.

My first notion was to get her onto her feet before she crushed her baby. I grabbed her around the neck, pulled and hauled. Of course, I only drove her deeper into panic. Her eyes opened wide and she set up a loud bawling as she wrestled against my efforts. Then a big hand landed on my shoulder.

"What the hell you think you're doing?" Byron said. I let go of the cow and he yanked me back. "She's already half crazy. Go get the truck and bring the winch."

I ran to where we'd left the pickup, my face burning—I felt angry at the cow and Byron equally. I returned with the calving winch, which looked something like a huge crossbow, and handed it to Byron. He braced the top of the T against the cow's hindquarters, then strapped the webbing of the winch cable to the calf. "You work the handle, but go easy," he said, reaching in alongside the half-born animal to find the other front leg. I turned the winch handle and he guided the calf out into the world.

The instant that calf hit the ground, the mother rolled onto her knees, then stood and ran off through the bush. "Forget her," Byron said. "She'll be okay. Let's get this one back to the yard." He picked up the animal, drenching his shirt front with birth slime, and carried it to the truck.

He tried everything he could think of to keep that calf alive, but by the end of the afternoon, the small creature just closed its eyes and stopped breathing. This time we carried the body together to the truck in a canvas tarp. Byron still hadn't changed his clothes, and half-heartedly brushed at his shirtsleeves as he stared at the dead animal. "You know what to do with this," he said. "I'm going to go clean up." Then he turned and walked off toward his cabin. I drove to a remote corner of the ranch where the roadside dropped away into the bush. This was our dead-calf dumping ground—the third time we'd used it since I'd started. I backed up to the shoulder, opened the tailgate and pushed the body as far down the slope as I could. The bears would soon smell the stink of its death and be along to finish the job.

Byron was silent on the drive back to my place that day.

When we got to the cabin, he shut off the engine and sat staring at his hands on the steering wheel. "I'm not pissed at you," he said, "if you're thinking that. You didn't do nothing wrong. I just hate losing an animal."

I wasn't sure if I should say anything or if I'd only make things more difficult by trying to explain that I'd done the best I could.

But before the moment dragged on too long, Becky was at Byron's window, grinning and smelling like a spruce forest. "Hey, you two cowboys," she said, "don't sit in this dirty truck all day. Come inside and see what I made for supper."

The following Friday, Byron suggested we drive to the Longbar Hall for a dance. I wasn't keen on socializing, but Byron explained that the best of the local country and bluegrass musicians—Trout Mountain String Band—would be playing, and I'd be missing an important Cariboo cultural event if I stayed home.

"Don't be so lazy, Porter," Becky said. "You might as well come with us."

"Come with you?" I said, realizing that something had been communicated between the two of them that I'd missed. We were sitting on the porch, watching the kids chase chickens around the greenhouse. I noticed Becky's hair was shining and that she was wearing her favourite dress.

"Yeah. I already told Byron I'd go with him."

When we'd lived in Edmonton, Becky had gone out with a couple of guys, but none of them lasted long. Either they got scared off by the way her attention would drift, or, if they seemed like bums, I put enough pressure on them to get out of her life before they did any harm to her. But this was different. I'd placed myself in the position of relying on Byron for work, and the two of them really seemed to like each other.

Now that I finally had to deal with the consequences I'd seen coming that day in town, I wasn't sure what to do.

So we went to the dance.

There I saw the woman from the tack shop, whose name was Nadine, and ended up dancing with her most of the night. "You're not much of a dancer," she told me, laughing. "But I think we can make something out of you."

"And who better to do the job?" I said.

The three of us shared a table with Nadine and her friends, but Becky wasn't planning to sit around. She had Byron swinging and kicking and humping his sorry self around the dance floor, song after song. At least he couldn't dance any better than me. The way he settled into his chair during the band's breaks, I could tell he wanted to take it easier, but he kept up with her.

After one set, when Becky and Nadine had gone off to the ladies' room, I asked him if he was having any fun. "Never danced so much in my life. Your sister," he said, and grinned at me, "she's like something I've never seen before."

"Yes," I said, "she's quite the gal, isn't she?" But all I could think about was that smirk on his face. I took a drink of my beer to have something to occupy my hands.

On my next day off, I went to visit Nadine in the store and she invited me home for supper. I brought her an armful of flowers; she cooked spicy Indian food. The air in the small apartment where she lived with her daughter was a strange mix of carnations and curry. That evening we started up a comfortable romance both of us knew would likely never get too complicated.

"I'm not planning to spend my life in Quesnel," I told her a few weeks later. We were lying on her bed, the night lit up with the unusual occurrence of a second full moon that month.

Nadine looked at me and smiled. Her dark hair fanned out on the pillow, and she pointed out the open window. "A blue moon," she said. "That's what they call this phenomenon. Appreciate it for what it is, but don't go making any prophecies about the future based on its appearance." She set her hand lightly on my chest. "And for what it's worth, neither am I."

By the end of the summer, Byron's presence was beginning to wear on me. His view of life was narrow and self-centred. The list of things that scratched against his contentment seemed to grow daily. He and Becky were spending a lot of time together, which meant I didn't get much of a break from him. And the tighter he got with her, the worse he treated me on the job. From the beginning I'd suspected he only tolerated me to draw her closer, and now he clearly felt he didn't need me any more. He made me tear down a feed shed I'd framed up, and start over on it. He'd frequently give me a long list of instructions, then take off in the truck, abandoning me on some remote part of the ranch. When he got back, if I hadn't accomplished everything he'd left me to do, he'd lose his temper and accuse me of slacking.

Haying, though, was the worst of it. Bad enough we had to work twelve-or thirteen-hour days in the heat of the Cariboo summer—"That's what they mean by 'Make hay while the sun shines,'" he said, an evil grin across his face as he sat above me on the shaded tractor seat. But as the day wore on and he began to worry that we wouldn't get all the hay in before the good weather quit on us, he'd speed up the baler and have me running along behind him, determined not to let him beat me.

One particularly hot afternoon, I was taking a break in the shade of an alder growing near the creek bed. I had a wet cloth over my forehead and had almost fallen asleep when Byron came along and roused me by kicking the soles of my boots. "Time's wasting," he said.

"Screw you," I answered. "I need a break or I'm going to get sunstroke."

"Look, when I hired you I told you this was man's work. If you're still just a boy, maybe you'd better start looking for some other line of employment."

I stood and faced him. "You know, Cossack, I'm getting a little tired of your mighty man act. You might want to think about who's doing most of the work around here. And if I quit and never have to see you again, you're the one who'll be left to take of care of things."

"Hah." He wiped the sweat from his face with his forearm. "And maybe you'd better get used to seeing even more of me, unless you're planning to leave this part of the country soon."

"What's that supposed to mean?" I said.

"Ask your sister," he said. "Now, you're already standing, so let's get back at it." He began to walk to the tractor.

I caught him and grabbed his arm. It felt like it was carved from some gnarled old pear branch. "What the fuck are you talking about?"

He just shook me off, climbed into the tractor seat and hit the ignition switch. "Talk's over," he said. "Time to earn your pay."

About two hours later, when a connector broke on the baler, we had to shut down early so Byron could take the piece in to the Pederson mill and get it welded. He dropped me at the top of the drive to the Sanctuary, and though I was tired, I felt lucky. I hurried to the cabin and found Becky shelling peas in the cool of the kitchen.

"What's going on with you and Byron?" I asked.

"Why don't you wash up?" she said. "You're dirty as a goat, but sweatier."

I slammed my hat on the table, sending a shower of green across the room. "Answer me, Becky."

She looked startled, then stared at the mess on the floor. "Porter, look what you've done to my work," she said. "Why are you so angry?"

She took her bowl and began to pick up peas as I told her what had happened that afternoon, and what Byron had said. I asked her what he'd meant. She suddenly began to cry, and I wished I'd thrown my hat somewhere else. "I'm sorry," I said. "Here, I'll help you."

"That's not it," she said. She sat on the floor with peas all around her. "It's a baby—I think there's a little baby growing in me."

The second thing that happened that week which helped direct my resolve came in the form of a letter from my Aunt Hannah. She wrote to let us know that she and Uncle Bernie had put Dad in some kind of a hospital. All along, I'd regularly sent him money, but his life had never improved after our Portage la Prairie days. Heavy drinking, too many drugs and near homelessness eventually wore him out. The Winnipeg police had picked him up for setting a fire in a dumpster behind the Assiniboine Hotel. He claimed the waiters there were Satan-worshippers and had been ordered by the dark prince to make his life miserable by refusing to serve him.

I got a ride up to town, made some phone calls, then went to see Nadine. It was already noon, so I asked if I could buy her lunch. "It's blue moon time," I said. In a booth at the Billy Barker restaurant I told her what was going on with Byron and Becky and me, that it was time for my sister and I to leave Quesnel, but first we needed her help. I spoke quietly so no one around us could hear me.

"A clinic?" she said. "There's only the hospital here, Porter. It's a small town."

"Will you help?"

"Of course," she said. "What does Byron have to say about this?"

I held her hand and looked out the window. "I think it's best if Byron isn't involved. It'll make it a lot easier on Becky," I said. "You're welcome to come with us to the coast," I said.

She squeezed my hand. "Thanks for asking."

In the end, it was Nadine who took Becky for the procedure, which is what they called it at the time. Becky had asked her to be there with her, and I felt relieved.

"I don't want Byron to know," my sister told Nadine. "I want him to think we left because we had to help Daddy." She gave Nadine a small box and asked her to pass it on to Byron after we were gone. Later, I asked Nadine to let me have a look at it. Inside, wrapped in a square of cloth that must have been cut from that dress she loved, was an old rabbit's foot keychain Mom had given Becky when we were kids.

I went to work that day, then told Byron I needed to take the afternoon off. We'd already managed to get all the hay stacked in the hay barns, so he graciously gave it to me. I didn't need a ride because I'd bought a green and white Ford pickup from a friend of Nadine's. On the way to the hospital, I stopped at the cabin to load our stuff in the back of the truck and tied it down under an orange plastic tarp.

Nadine and Becky were waiting for me inside the hospital entrance. I wheeled my sister out to the truck and set her up in the passenger seat against a pile of blankets and coats. She seemed groggy and didn't say much; she had the look of someone recently arrived from a long and difficult journey. As I buckled her in, she closed her eyes and went to sleep. I thanked Nadine for her help, promised I'd write. Though I said it with the common, half intention of: "I'm glad you came into my life," we actually did keep in touch for a couple of years before I lost track of her.

I pointed the truck south and headed for Vancouver. Despite the grieving such a departure demanded, I felt happy to be on our way. I imagined better things lay hidden for both of us, that all we had to do was recognize them and they would be ours.

I didn't want the noise of the radio, so I drove in silence until, somewhere near Williams Lake, Becky opened her eyes. "Stop the truck, Porter," she said, her voice calm. "I need to get out."

I pulled over to the gravel, thinking she had to go to the bathroom and hoping there wouldn't be any problem for her. Before I could kill the engine, Becky was out of the truck, spilling blankets into the ditch as she climbed through the grass and fireweed, over a split-board fence, and disappeared into the brush.

The truck was on an incline, so I had to find a rock to wedge behind a tire—I didn't trust the emergency brake on that old vehicle. Then I climbed the fence and went through the bush. From the light beyond, I could tell there was a clearing on the other side, and I stopped at its edge to witness probably the strangest sight I've ever seen.

The meadow was a thick carpet of honey-toned grass, foxtails and tansy, radiant in the late afternoon light. And there in the middle stood two ash-coloured birds with long necks and red-capped heads: sandhill cranes. The birds strode—stiff-legged like trance walkers—toward my sister, who simply waited for them with her hands held forward, palms up. They approached her cautiously, then stopped a few steps away from her. I watched and realized Becky was talking to them. Finally, she turned and the cranes seemed startled, as if a spell had been broken. I watched those large animals, wings beating and necks tucked in, rise into the sky and move gracefully, like a vision, away from us.

She dropped her hands and looked at me. I could see she'd been crying, but she smiled and said, "Let's go now, Porter." Her face was relaxed and empty of the fatigue I'd seen there earlier. She didn't mention the cranes or try to explain what had happened. I was thankful she seemed okay, so I didn't ask, but I wondered exactly what I'd witnessed and what Becky had said to the cranes, and if this moment was, in fact, something I would ever truly understand.

On the way back from the Elias, I take a detour past the Alberta Wheat Pool elevators and along the south shore of the inlet. I park near a three-high stack of shipping containers marked "Astra International"—dark blue with a spray of stars across each. It feels strange to have a wall of night on one side of me while the mid-morning sun lights the mountains in the north.

I think about Becky and wonder, as I have almost daily since leaving Quesnel, if I did the right thing for her, or if I should have left her with Byron to a life among the trees and fireweed. Wonder who it was I'd been protecting. Of course I have no answer. What I arrive at each time is the reality of my sister, half lost in her own thoughts, talking to birds and smiling to herself as if she knows something she won't tell.

I consider all the miles we've travelled together, the ground we covered since those days on the prairies. How much energy I've put into being more of a parent than a brother to her. I've always wanted the best life for both of us.

When the noon whistle blows from some worksite on the docks, I start the car and drive home. I imagine Melanie will be feeding Katrina now, and suddenly I'm hungry. I want to be home, to hold my daughter, to sit at a chair in the kitchen with my family and plan the rest of the day. A simple enough thing.